Karma Dog

Unleashing Redemption

David Homick

"No human being is beyond redemption."
Mahatma Gandhi

Chapter One

My entire world changed in an instant. The last thing I remember is a blinding light. Everything else is pretty sketchy.

Where am I? How did I get here? It's so dark I can't see my hand in front of my face. "Somebody turn on a light. My name is Mitchell Patrick Westcott III, and I demand to be told where I am and why I'm here. You want money? How much? My father will pay your ransom. Just let me go."

The blackness transforms into a dense gray fog that swirls around me. Light creeps in at the corners of my vision until a blurry picture takes shape. The moment my eyes adjust, my nightmare begins.

A huge dog stares down at me. At least, I think it's a dog. It might be a pig. Others are here, but they're much smaller and look more like puppies than pigs.

I'm not a dog person. Never have been, never will be. I squeeze my eyes shut and open them. The big one continues to stare. That's one ugly dog. Either that dog is ten feet tall, or I've shrunk to the size of a baby squirrel. When I see the wrinkled ball of fur that has replaced my magnificent twenty-four-year-old body, I realize the latter is true.

I scream, but all that comes out is a little yip. *What happened to my voice?*

Everyone is staring.

Show's over. Go on, get out of here.

The big dog, who appears to be in charge, licks me—yuck! She tells me it's okay. But it isn't. None of this is okay. It smells in here. I want to go home and throw back a couple of glasses of Macallan single malt. Clearly, that's not going to happen.

I close my eyes. *Concentrate, Mitch!* I'm disoriented. This is a joke or a bad dream, or perhaps karma has a wicked sense of humor. Where was I before I woke up in this stinking cardboard box? Fuzzy images float through my mind like clouds in a summer sky. *Focus!*

I'm banging on a door. No one answers. Whose door is this? Why am I here? I'm upset. Banging and banging. A stranger stops me and says the tenant, Ashley, has moved out and left no forwarding address. He asks if my name is Mitch, and when I acknowledge, he hands me a letter. I tear it open.

It's from Ashley. She says she's sorry, but she needs to go. The last line says, *please don't try to find me.*

I need more information, but the memory is fading. *Wait.* I'm in my car now. I've had a few drinks and I'm driving too fast. Then the light. Then darkness. Then THIS. One moment I'm a man, and the next I'm a... a dog? I let out a string of expletives that would make a truck driver blush.

I don't know where my car is, and even if I could see over the dash and reach the pedals, I'd need opposable thumbs to hold the steering wheel. Obviously, I didn't drive here. These stupid little paws at the end of my arms—do dogs even have arms?—are useless.

I struggle to walk on these things as I make my way to the farthest corner of the room, which isn't a room at all but a cardboard box, and hunker down. The big dog follows me. She's talking, but not talking. I hear her thoughts. It's time to eat, she says and walks away.

I'm not a dog. I don't belong here.

I'm hungry, but I can't eat. I need time to think, to find a way out of this nightmare. Perhaps if I can remember how I got here, I can figure a way out.

Wait. I remember that name on the note—Ashley. We were dating. I used to go through women like a kid goes through crayons, but Ash was different. I thought she might be the one. I think she dumped me, but that's impossible. Mitchell Patrick Westcott III is always the dumper, never the dumped.

The longer I sit, the stronger the ache in my stomach grows, but I don't see any food. What do dogs eat? Ashley had a dog named Rufus, and he was a big, slobbering pain in the ass. I normally had a no-pet rule, but Ash was hot, so I made an exception. She must have fed him, but I never paid much attention to what he ate.

The big dog reclines, and the little ones rush toward her, climbing over one another to get a front-row seat. Four of them—a chaotic tangle of heads, feet, and fur, jockey for position.

I watch from my corner. *What's going on?*

The one at the back of the scrum turns. *Can't talk now, time to eat.*

Finally, some good news. I wait for someone to set a bowl of food in front of me. Rufus had a big bowl with his name on the side. I don't know what was in it, but he seemed to like it. At this point, I'll eat just about anything.

I wait. And wait. *The service in this place is terrible.*

Hey, dummy, one of them calls. *You'd better get over here if you want to eat.*

Dummy? I charge the pile and jump on his back. He throws me off, and I run back into the fray. As I bounce around like a furry ping-pong ball, I realize what's going on. There are no bowls. *You've got to be kidding me!* The big dog is the food.

I wriggle my way out of the pile and watch the mayhem from a distance. This can't be happening. I need some real food. There must be a way out of here. After a quick check of the perimeter turns up nothing, I get a running start and crash into the wall, hoping to break through.

After the third unsuccessful attempt, the big dog speaks. *Stop that and come eat with the others.*

I'm dizzy from smashing my head against the wall and can no longer ignore the pain in my stomach. I have a decision to make. Desperate times require desperate measures. Reluctantly, I wiggle my way to the front of the pile, close my eyes, and suck.

The process feels surprisingly natural. The warm liquid tastes sweet and soothes the ache in my stomach. Mitch had certainly ingested worse things.

After I have my fill, I stagger away, feeling somewhat intoxicated. I return to my corner and recline. The others mingle, but I'm not ready to embrace the puppy life. Whoever said "happiness is a warm puppy" probably didn't live in a box with them.

I study the furry mass that's replaced my body and stick my head down between my hind legs, something I could never do until today. How had I not noticed this before? A dog's private parts aren't very private. I guess I just assumed they would be there.

And the hits just keep on coming. As if becoming a dog wasn't bad enough, I had become a female dog.

Chapter Two

So, how did I get here, wherever here is? Did I die and go to hell? This surely isn't heaven. And why a dog? I don't even like dogs. What could I possibly have done to deserve this? Okay, I could have been nicer to Rufus. But if this is some form of cosmic retribution, there must be more to it than that. Maybe this is a bad dream. Nightmare is more like it. *Wake up, Mitch!* I can't pinch myself with these stupid paws, but I can bite.

Ouch! Still here. Okay, if not a dream, then what?

Another memory surfaces. I burst into my father's study to find his smug face where it always is, behind his desk. He knows why I'm there. He's done something... again. Another attempt to control my life and make me just like him. I refuse to let that happen.

Unwilling to admit to anything, he changes the subject. Apparently, the school has contacted him again with some rather unsavory news regarding my recent performance. One more disappointment, in a long line of disappointments. I've stopped trying to please the man. He threatens to freeze my credit cards until my grades improve, and I tell him to be fruitful and multiply, but not in those words. Mother pleads with me not to leave angry, but I've made up my mind. I never want to see that man again.

Inside my car, I let out a tirade of the things I wish I'd been able to say to him. I drive to Ashley's favorite hangout, the Cocktail Cove, hoping to find her there.

By ten o'clock I haven't seen her, but I've seen the bottom of my glass a half dozen times. I order one more for courage, pay my tab, and leave. Outside, I'm confronted by an angry patron who doesn't like the way I parked. My car is taking up two spaces—standard operating procedure when you drive a two-hundred-thousand-dollar car. I flip him off and light up my tires on the way out of the parking lot.

My memory falters, and I'm back in the box with a bunch of smelly dogs. The big one must know what's going on. Maybe I can get some more information from her.

Hey, Big Dog, we need to talk.

I'm your mother. A little respect would be nice.

First, my mother's name is Meredith. And second, I need to get back.

Back? Back where?

Back to Westport, Connecticut. Back to my life. I'm not a dog.

So I've heard.

My name is Mitch Westcott. I'm twenty-four years old. I'm a person, a man who has lots of money and drives a Porsche 911 Turbo S. I don't belong here.

I see. It looks to me like you are neither a person nor a man.

I hear a few giggles from the peanut gallery.

It may not look like it at the moment, but I assure you I am. I take as deep a breath as my little puppy lungs will allow. *Now, if you don't mind, I need to speak to the person in charge.*

More giggles.

That would be me. I'm your mother.

I said the PERSON in charge. There must be someone around here who walks on two legs. Wait... I get it now. Someone is trying to teach me a lesson. Like in the movies—Cash from The Family Man *or Clarence from* It's a Wonderful Life. *I need to speak to whoever concocted this nightmare.*

She shakes her head. *I can see you're going to be a handful.*

Speaking of hands, how am I supposed to do anything with these? I sit back and hold up my front paws. *Where are my thumbs?*

Her laugh seems a bit condescending. *I get along just fine, and you will too.*

I retreat to my corner to sort things out but get nowhere. Memories of the events leading up to my incarceration in this box are returning, but still sketchy.

The big one, who I refuse to call Mom or Mother or Mama, wanders over and licks my back when I'm not looking.

I pull away. *Really?*

What's the matter? I can see you're upset. I'm just trying to comfort you.

She sounds sincere, and my muscles relax. *I'm confused. Can you tell me what's going on?*

That's better. I'm not sure, but you aren't the first of my pups with an attitude.

You mean there have been more like me?

I had one about a year ago. Kept insisting he was John from Boston. Stirred up a lot of trouble.

Okay. Now we're getting somewhere. What happened to him?

Eventually, a human took him away.

Where'd they take him?

She shrugs. *I never know what happens to them.*

That's rough. Why do you stay here?

I don't know where else to go.

What if you stopped having puppies?

I'm sure they'd put me down.

Yikes! Do they ever kill the pups?

Only if they don't get sold.

What?! We're for sale?

That's the whole point. It's a business. I'm only good to them as long as I'm pumping out pups they can sell. She sighs. *The demand for pugs like us comes and goes.*

Excuse me. Pigs?

Not pigs, pugs.

What's that?

It's a dog breed.

I'm sure it's no coincidence that it's only one letter off from pig.

We're all pugs in this box.

About this box. It's a little cramped, don't you think? You need to talk to a realtor about finding a bigger place.

I had a litter of seven in here once.

That's nice, but let's get back to MY problem. I need to get out of here. I'm not a dog, or at least, I didn't use to be.

I'm afraid that ship has sailed. You're a dog now.

No way I'm doing this, but I don't think anyone here can help. I need to get back to Westport.

An awkward silence hangs in the air.

This is unacceptable. There's been a huge mistake that needs to be corrected as soon as possible.

I know you feel that way, but you need to get used to the idea that this is your life now.

Are there any humans around here?

The only one I ever see is Alice. She takes care of us.

My stomach rumbles. *Perhaps she can show me where the toilets are.*

If you mean where we do our business, that would be outside. We're expected to hold it until Alice comes and gets us.

Is there a bathroom out there, or are we supposed to just drop a deuce out in the yard with everyone watching?

Bathrooms are for humans. This is more... natural. You'll get used to it.

I glance over at the other four, tumbling around in a pile. *Hellooo... You're not listening. I AM A HUMAN.*

You are a puppy, and the sooner you get with the program and act like one, the smoother this will go.

Just so you know, I'm not used to being told what to do.

Good luck with that.

A human head appears above the side of the box. Alice's, I presume. Perhaps SHE did this to me and can right this wrong.

If you don't undo whatever spell you've cast...

Big dog looks at me. *Humans can't hear us.*

What? I'm getting the feeling that finding a way out of this mess isn't going to be easy.

CHAPTER THREE

Time loses its meaning. Days and weeks bleed into each other. I'm trapped within a body that lacks the privileges and entitlements I once enjoyed, with no phone or other means of keeping track of time. I have memories of Mitch's past, but here in this bizarre world, the past and future don't exist.

I notice other changes. My sense of smell is a hundred times better than Mitch's ever was, which is a double-edged sword. It also worries me that I've begun referring to myself in the third person. I'm losing my grip on reality, if there is such a thing anymore. Unfortunately, my daily attempts to breach the walls of this prison are unsuccessful.

Two of my siblings are gone, their whereabouts unknown. The three little pigs, as I refer to the rest of us, are growing and eating solid food now. We've moved from our box into a much larger cage-like structure. While we spend most of our time roughhousing and playing like clueless children, I have moments of clarity when I worry about how long Alice will put up with us before she cuts her losses. It's hard to let go of life, even if it's not the one you envisioned yourself living.

One of the other pups, I'll call him Bad Dog, becomes aggressive and goes all Mike Tyson on us. The other one, I'll call him Good Dog, suffers a nasty injury defending his sister, otherwise known as me. The next morning, Good Dog is gone. With no one left to defend me, I brace for another attack and register a formal complaint with Big Dog. I smell fear as she silently licks my back, so I let her. I think she's saying goodbye.

Later that day, Alice reaches in and scoops up Bad Dog and me.

News flash, Alice. I'm not a dog. Where are you taking us? I need to make a phone call.

Big Dog watches with sad eyes. She taught me about the sad eyes. They generally have a positive effect on humans. Lowering the head and blinking produces a similar out-come. I have an idea what is going on here, so I look at Alice with the saddest eyes I can muster. She looks away, and I realize I'm a death row dog. The fear I smell is mine.

Bad Dog had it coming, but why me? I did nothing wrong. The humans control my destiny. Not just the executioner who carries me outside to the firing squad, but the humans that are too good for a less than perfect dog. They come and look into my box and snicker like I'm some kind of sideshow freak, then put their money down on another, prettier pooch.

Alice drops Bad Dog when he bites her hand. I squirm in her other hand, hoping to take advantage of the distraction, but she holds tight. She gives me to a man with bad breath and a sour look on his face, then chases after Bad Dog. Alice will win this skirmish. Humans always do.

I understand now that dogs don't get to choose their destiny. People make all the choices. This is difficult for me to accept. I'm used to being in control. Father will tell you otherwise. True, he held the purse strings, but for better or worse, Mitch was his own man. This caused a rift that remains to this day.

Sourpuss sets me down on the front seat of his truck, then leaves. I stand on my hind legs and look out the window, but don't see a firing squad, just this rusty old pickup truck. Where is he taking me? He returns with Bad Dog and throws him in the back.

I watch Bad Dog roll around in the truck bed as we drive off. Wherever Good Dog is, I hope he's seeing this. *Payback's a bitch, isn't it?* I laugh, which sounds like a bark.

"Shut up."

I zip it and sit on the seat. I'm glad Mitch isn't here. If anyone ever saw him riding in a junker like this, he'd be humiliated. There, I did it again. *I'm Mitch! ME, not HE.*

We drive for a while. It could be a mile or it could be twenty. We pull over to the side of the road, and I check on Bad Dog. He paces, shaken from the ride. I try to feel sorry for him, but it's not easy.

"Stay here," Sourpuss says as he exits the vehicle.

I have no choice. Paws aren't made for opening doors. Besides, where would I go? We appear to be in the middle of nowhere.

Sourpuss picks up Bad Dog and throws him into the thick brush that grows along the road. *Yikes!* That's worse than a firing squad. He'll starve out here and die a slow, agonizing death. Sadly, Mitch had considered taking Rufus for a ride on more than one occasion. Okay, so empathy wasn't his strong suit. Animals had been inconsequential creatures existing on life's periphery, not worthy of the devotion and fuss others seemed to bestow upon them. Funny how a change of perspective can affect one's attitudes and values.

I watch Sourpuss as we drive off. This could go one of two ways. Either I'm next, or he brought me along to teach me a lesson by showing me what happens to dogs that misbehave. Either way, he's got my attention.

If I still had my voice, I might be able to reason with this heartless SOB. If that didn't work, I'm sure a handful of cash would change his mind. He pulls over again, and I know which way this is going.

He reaches over and opens the door. "No offense. It's just business." He pushes me out and closes the door.

The words echo in my ears, but they're not his words, they're mine. Well, technically, they're Mitch's. The truck speeds off in a cloud of dust and stones. I scramble out of the way before it rolls over my hind legs.

Not cool! I bark. Fear grips my heart as the truck recedes into the distance, and I can't shake the feeling this might somehow be my fault. Payback's a bitch.

Chapter Four

I don't have time to play the blame game. I'm hungry, and there's no one out here to bring me my dinner. Mitch never went hungry. I'd love to have some of the food he so carelessly threw away.

I walk along the road, looking for food and shelter. The area is desolate, and I have no idea where I am. Nothing but woods and more woods. I've heard of people living in places like this, but I don't see any houses. I have no choice but to keep on walking on these little legs that make it nearly impossible to get anywhere.

I keep moving, up one hill and down another. My stomach aches and my feet, or paws or whatever they're called, are numb. The wind whispers through the trees, their leaves rustling like distant voices. I hear my father's among them. "You never listen. I say zig and you zag. How much disappointment can one father take? When you end up alone and penniless, don't come crying to me. On second thought, do that, so I can say I told you so."

I let out a whine and berate myself for it. Mitch never cried. Do dogs cry? Before I find out, I shake it off the way Big Dog taught us to shake when we get wet. I miss Big Dog for a moment before I muster up enough courage to stop wallowing in my predicament. I miss Mitch, too. He was a lot of things, but a quitter wasn't one of them, so I keep moving forward.

There's a clearing up ahead and a mailbox on a post at the edge of the road. A burst of energy pushes me forward. After wandering for two days and spending a night alone in the woods, which was the scariest thing I've ever done, I find civilization at last.

Behind the house, I notice an overstuffed trash can. I head-butt the can hard enough that one of the bags falls onto the ground. Like a savage beast, I tear it open and rummage through it to find table scraps and leftovers that had likely been neglected in the fridge. I don't care. Not knowing where my next meal might come from, I devour every morsel.

Mitchell Patrick Westcott III is eating garbage from a can. What would dear old Dad say if he could see me now? No time to linger with such thoughts. I need to keep moving.

At first, the houses are close together, like a hamlet or small village. I don't recognize the area, and I'm unable to determine how far I've traveled or in which direction. After a while, the distances between the houses grow, and I spend a few nights sleeping in the woods.

I manage to survive another week before I happen upon a house set way back in the woods. My stomach twisting with hunger, I follow the long driveway toward the house. I smell other dogs, lots of them, and proceed with caution. Hillbillies with guns and banjos and lots of dogs live back in the woods. The house should have been condemned years ago. There's a barn a couple of hundred feet from the house, and I make my way toward it.

I hear barking from inside as I approach. They know I'm here and are calling to me, telling me this is a dreadful place and I should run. I tell them I'm so hungry I don't have the strength to run. They direct me around back to a hole in the wall where I can enter.

The air inside is heavy with the smell of fear and sadness and bodily secretions. A dozen dogs, each one chained to a stake in the ground, are the only occupants. I approach the nearest dog, and we, you now, sniff each other. He has little food, but offers me some. It smells like sewage, but I'm so hungry, so I choke it down.

I'm Clyde. What's your name?

I... I guess I don't have one. I hadn't needed one up to this point, but now I'm amazed at the depths to which I've sunk. Nameless, homeless, and eating what might be raw sewage in a place that looks and smells like a canine version of hell.

Whoever you are, you shouldn't be here.

Roger that, but I have nowhere else to go and can't walk another step even if I did. Can I crash here for the night?

I hear a ruckus coming from another room. *What's that?*

That's Raptor, the reason you need to leave.

Raptor?

Fight dog. The two humans who live in the house raise dogs to fight other dogs for money. They starve him and beat him to keep him mean.

I glance around the room. *What about you guys?*

We're practice dummies. Every few days, they throw one of us in the ring with Raptor so he can practice ripping us to shreds. All the blood and guts get him primed for the main event.

That's just evil. Sadly, Mitch had attended a dog fight once. He won two hundred dollars, bought a round of drinks for his friends, and didn't think twice about it.

Clyde motions toward a stake with an empty chain on the other side of the room. *That was Iggy's spot until this afternoon.*

Do they ever come back?

He hangs his head and paws at the dirt.

How do they pick who goes next?

It's random. We never know who's next.

And I thought I had it bad. *Here's what nobody seems to understand. I'm not a dog, I'm a person. My name is Mitch Westcott. Perhaps you've heard of me.*

Clyde looks at me like I have three heads.

I drive a Porsche 911 Turbo S, and I can buy and sell those two yahoos and their prize fighting dog a hundred times over.

A man's voice calls out from the other side of the wall just before Raptor yelps in pain. The barn door opens and another man steps inside. I freeze. He's a hillbilly, all right. His dirty overalls are only buckled on one side, and his ratty hair hangs to his shoulders.

I move my legs, but my paws scratch at the concrete floor and slide in every direction. Before I can get any traction, Gomer has his arm around me and lifts me up. More than a few of his teeth are missing, but apparently his eyesight is perfect. His partner, who looks like the freakish banjo player in the movie *Deliverance*, joins him.

Gomer holds me up in the air. "Looky what I found."

Banjo shakes his head. "Too bad we can't use her. We agreed only males. We ain't barbarians."

They laughed like a couple of drunken hyenas.

You heard the man. Put me down. You idiots have no idea who you're dealing with.

"She's a little too young, anyway. Maybe we should get her out of here before these other dogs get their horns up. Boys'll be boys, ya know?"

"That gives me an idea. We keep her around for another month, and when she's old enough, we use her as a reward."

Banjo scratches his head. "How's that?"

"Whenever Raptor wins, we let him have his way with her after the fight."

Wait a minute. That's a terrible idea. I definitely did not want to be on the receiving end of such a transaction.

"You're not as dumb as you look, brother." He slapped his thigh. "Raptor will never lose another fight as long as he lives."

The hyenas are back.

"We gotta give her a name."

Gomer holds me up to his face. He smells like a brewery. "She looks like she got hit in the face with a frying pan."

I want to spit in his eye, but I don't know how.

Banjo smiles his freak-show smile. "Let's call her Panny."

"Settled. Tie her up in Iggy's spot."

He nods and secures the chain around my neck. "You and Raptor are gonna make a cute couple."

I'm whining again. I should have listened to Clyde and got the hell out of this place while I had the chance.

Clarence, or whoever you are, now would be a good time to show yourself. If you're trying to teach me a lesson, you've succeeded. Time to take me home, back to my real life.

More whining. *Clarence? Cash? Anybody?*

CHAPTER FIVE

The night is cold and lonely. I shiver, but it's not in response to the cold air. The mournful sounds of a dozen dogs mix with mine and chill me to the bone. I attempt to free myself, only to rub my neck raw against the metal collar.

In the morning, Banjo feeds us some unappealing slop and tells Clyde he's on deck for today's death match. I hang my head, feeling sad and helpless. Mitch had never mastered the art of compassion, but he had earned a black belt in judo. I assume Raptor is not a finesse fighter, so I give Clyde some pointers on how he might use his opponent's aggression and momentum against him. He's grateful for the encouragement, but I can sense his overwhelming fear mixed with resignation.

The morning wears on, and all we can do is wait. Suddenly, everyone is up and stirring. Something is happening outside—vehicle sounds and multiple voices. I pray the fight is not about to begin.

Clyde hunkers down in a defensive position and looks at me for help. *Okay, I believe you. Help me out here, Mitch.*

I look away. I have my own problems. Why should I care what happens to some stray dog I didn't know before yesterday? But inexplicably, a part of me cares.

My heart skips a beat as light rushes into the gloom, illuminating two sheriff's deputies in the doorway. The cavalry has arrived in the nick of time, just like in the movies. The room fills with joyous noise as the captives bark and strain against their chains, eager to show their appreciation to their saviors.

The deputies bury their noses in their arms in response to the dreadful smell, which I guess I'd gotten used to.

"This is disgusting."

"Let's get these poor animals some fresh air."

One by one, they release our bonds and lead us outside where they give us water from a hose. Everyone behaves, grateful to be free. My human side trusts these deputies will take us to a better place. My animal instincts have me drinking until I can't drink any more, unsure of where we are going and when we might eat or drink again.

The deputies take Gomer and Banjo away in handcuffs. I want to bite their ankles as they pass. A van pulls up and I overhear the deputies talking. My nose isn't the only thing that works better. They plan to take us to Animal Control. I don't like the sound of that, but I smell food when the back doors open. A giant bag of kibble had been dumped into troughs on either side of the back of the van, and we jockey for position like shoppers waiting for the doors to open on Black Friday.

The van drives off and we tumble like dominoes, but no one seems to care. I ask Clyde what he knows about Animal Control.

I think they pick up strays and put them in animal shelters.

I ask him if he's ever been to a shelter.

I did some time there once. It's better than where we just came from, but it still feels like a prison. If you stay there too long, they put you down.

I know what that means. *Why would anyone stay there too long?*

If no one claims you or wants to adopt you.

I'm pretty sure neither of those things is in my future. *I can't go there.*

Where will you go?

Like I said, I'm not a dog. I need to find whoever did this to me and have them undo it. I have a nice home in Westport and lots of money. You can come with me.

Clyde raises an eye but says nothing.

I need to break out.

He tilts his head. *How do you plan to do that? We're in a moving truck.*

You with me or not?

He hesitates. *I think I'll take my chances at the shelter.*

Easy for you to say. I shove my face into his. *You don't look like THIS.*

Clyde has no comment, which speaks volumes.

Did you forget? Banjo calls me Panny because I look like I lost a fight with a frying pan.

If you ask me, Clyde says, shaking his head, *he's in no position to be making fun of anyone's looks.*

Despite my frustration, I smile. I don't know what that looks like on the outside, but it feels like a smile on the inside. *Back there, when you said you believed me about not being a dog...*

Look, man, I thought I was going to die. At that point, you believe anything you think might save you.

I shake off my disappointment, weave my way to the back, and prepare to make my move. The van stops and I hear the driver get out. I take a deep breath when the back door latch clicks. Timing is everything. In *The Art of War*, Sun Tzu says confrontation is done directly; victory is gained by surprise. I tuck my head and launch myself at the unsuspecting deputy.

She falls backwards, and I land on top of her. She's a cute one. It feels good to be on top of a woman again, but I don't have time to linger. *Rain check?* I take off and don't look back. My little legs are pumping at top speed, like I'm trying to catch a squirrel on roller skates.

Shelters are for suckers. Sorry, Clyde.

My size allows me to do things I could have only dreamed of doing in the past with the police in pursuit—shimmy under a parked truck, squeeze through a fence, hide in tall weeds. Done, done, and done. The last time I was in weeds this tall, I was hitting out of the deep rough on the seventh hole at Longshore. I raise my head above the weeds to get a look. They've given up the chase and are busy herding the other dogs into the building.

I'm alone and on my own again, but it's better than prison. Food and rudimentary shelter are more readily available in the city, so there's that. But I don't know where to go or what to do. I need money, a speaking voice, and opposable thumbs. Oh yeah, and my car.

Chapter Six

Who am I kidding? I'm never going to drive my car again. I know that sounds ridiculous coming from a dog. Dogs don't own cars, and they certainly don't drive them. I wonder what happened to my car and who's driving it now.

I take another look. The van is gone. I hunker down and a memory surfaces. I'm drunk and pissed and shouldn't be driving, but I'm breaking my land speed record in the Porsche on a dark country road. I lose control on a curve and cross the yellow line. Bright lights blind me for a second and I overturn the wheel. The Porsche is airborne and busting through tree branches. Then the lights go out.

I roll over on my back in the weeds and stare up at the clouds. That might explain why Mitch is no longer with us in human form. It's hard to believe he's gone, just like that. I'd never given much thought to what happens when we die. In school, they taught us about heaven and hell, but this doesn't fit. I haven't seen any angels, and with the possible exception of Gomer and Banjo, no demons either. Perhaps this is some place in between. But why am I a dog? I don't even like dogs. It makes no sense.

To add insult to injury, I turn into THIS. Why couldn't I be one of those dogs all the women think are so cute? Like that dog, Marley, in the movies. I'm not saying that Mitch watched dog movies. It was movie night at Ashley's. Her choice.

Big Dog said I was a pug. I'd never heard of such a thing or seen an uglier dog. I have my whole miserable life ahead of me, listening to the mean dogs call me Pugzilla, or This Little Puggy, or Shit Face. I suddenly identify with all the misfits Mitch and his friends mocked in high school, and don't like how it feels to be on the receiving end of such torture. I shake it off. What goes around comes around, I guess. But you have to admit, this is taking it a bit too far.

I roll over onto my feet and decide I've wallowed enough for one day. I have more important things to do. A lecture from Psych class surfaces—Maslow's hierarchy of needs. I'm at the bottom of the pyramid right now. I need to satisfy my physiological needs, like food and shelter, before moving on to higher needs like safety, love, and self-esteem. I have a long way to go to reach that last one.

The first order of business is lunch. I'm pretty sure it's lunchtime. My stomach agrees. I'm in a city now, but I don't know which one. I smell water, a river perhaps, and head in that direction, cutting a wide berth around the building where they took the other dogs. The river appears when I round a bend in the road. On the other side is a familiar sight—the Black Duck. I've docked there and had lunch a few times. Traffic flows overhead on the I-95 bridge over the Saugatuck River.

Hallelujah. I'm still in Westport. I know people here. Perhaps someone can help me. Wait. What am I thinking? No one I know would care about a stray dog, especially one who looks like me. I should have made better friends.

First things first, I need to cross the river. The food at the Black Duck is pretty good, and I hear restaurants throw away almost as much food as people eat. Can dogs swim? I don't want to chance it. I-95 is too dangerous, but there's a railroad bridge a hundred yards downriver. I amble along the rocky shoreline, in no particular hurry.

I hear dogs barking, and not in a good way. They're getting louder, and I panic. Suddenly, three of the biggest, scariest dogs I've ever seen are charging toward me, tongues hanging out over bared teeth. I don't know what their problem is, but if I had to guess, I'd say it's me.

So far, my life has not been all sunshine and rainbows, but I don't want to go out like this. Running isn't my strong suit, but it sure beats getting eaten by a pack of wild dogs. I have about a five-second head start if I take off now. Every second

I hesitate brings me closer to certain death. I run toward the bridge as fast as adrenaline and my little legs will take me.

They quickly close the gap. I'll never be able to outrun them all the way up the embankment to the bridge, so I head underneath and keep running. No time to look back. If I had a normal length tail, I'm sure they'd be biting it.

Among the debris along the shoreline under the bridge is a cardboard box the size of a compact car sitting up against the abutment. A man's head pops up from inside like a jack-in-the-box. He surveys the impending carnage with wide eyes.

I cry out. *Help!* I know he can't understand me, but I don't know what else to do.

His eyes are wild as he rushes out of the box with a base-ball bat and steps in front of the approaching marauders. They slam on the brakes when he raises the bat.

"Back off!"

The dogs hold their ground, growling and showing their teeth. I duck behind the back of the box and peek around the corner.

"I mean it." The man, I'll call him Jack, cocks the bat like he's about to send all three of them into the river with one mighty swing.

They mill around impatiently, deciding if I'm worth it.

Jack stamps his foot in their direction, and they disperse. He sets the bat down, and I emerge from my refuge, wheezing and snorting and shaking like a squirrel on caffeine.

"Are you okay?"

For the moment. You think they'll be back? I realize he can't understand me, so I bark and wag.

He steps back into the box and gestures for me to follow. "Come on in. I don't get much company out here."

Much? I'd bet money I'm the first.

My senses tingle with a mixture of curiosity and trepidation. He saved my life, so there's that. I step inside his home, a term I use loosely, and he smiles. He has little more than the tattered clothes on his back, and his weathered face bears the unmistakable signs of hardship. If I ever saw this long-haired, bearded hobo waving a baseball bat at me, I'd hightail it out of there quicker than those jackals who were chasing me.

Inside, his features soften and his eyes glisten with an unexpected warmth. The only thing sinister about this guy is his smell, which I assume is not uncommon for someone living in a box under a bridge. I consider my situation and realize I'm in no position to cast aspersions, but I remain cautious.

I'd heard about homeless people but never actually met one. He looks the part. His mismatched clothes, unshaven face, dirty hair give the impression he hasn't had a proper home for some time.

His face is oddly familiar, and that bothers me. Mitch wouldn't have touched this guy with a ten-foot pole. Did he ever see him in the street? Did he laugh and tell him to get a job? It wouldn't have been the first time he'd done something like that.

This place has much more room than the box I used to live in. I can't believe I'm saying this, but I'm envious. He has little in the way of possessions—a worn mattress, a beanbag chair that has seen better days, a pile of plastic bags filled with God knows what, and of course, a baseball bat.

"Come here, girl," he says from his chair and waves me over.

I'm still getting used to the whole *girl* thing. I'm happy to keep my distance, but something I can't control moves me toward him. Apparently, my inner Mitch is at odds with my outer dog.

He strokes my back and scratches behind my ears. I'm not used to men putting their hands on me, but it feels good, so I lean into it. I need help, and so far, this hobo is the only person who has shown any interest.

"You're still a pup. What are you doing wandering around alone down here?"

You wouldn't believe me if I told you, which I can't do because I can only bark. But that's temporary. My name is Mitch, and I live right here in Westport.

"You must be homeless, like me."

I have a home. Here in Westport. If you take me there, maybe we can straighten this mess out.

He holds my head in both hands and pulls my face up to his. His breath could knock a buzzard off a shit wagon. I hold mine.

"Being homeless sure teaches you about life, doesn't it?"

I exhale. *Wait! You did this to me? I don't need any more lessons. I demand you undo whatever spell you've cast.*

"You learn to accept the hand you've been dealt and make the best of it."

News flash. I'm not a dog. I'm not learning anything.

"You look like a dog I had a few years back."

I don't care about YOUR dog. I care about THIS dog, who used to be a man. I'm Mitchell Patrick Westcott III, and I want my life back!

He holds me up higher, giving me the once over. "Yup, spittin' image."

You had a dog that looked like me? Really? He has my condolences. I consider the significance of his remark. This guy obviously doesn't have a problem with the way I look. It's nice to take a break from the abuse and name calling.

"His name was Punch." He laughs. "He looked like someone punched him in the face."

Aaand... we're back. Like I said, I'm not a dog.

"My name's Jim."

Okay. JIM-in-the-box. I stand corrected. I'm starving, Jim. You got anything to eat?

"You need a name. I think I'm gonna call you Punch Jr."

I glare at him and let out a long, low growl.

"I guess you don't like it. How about if I just call you Junior?"

Maybe this is a bad idea. I study Jim for a moment, deciding if I should cut my losses and run. He scratches behind my ears, and I melt a little.

"You look hungry." He stands. "Come on, Junior. Let's go get us something to eat."

Perhaps I'll reserve judgment until after lunch.

Chapter Seven

I follow him up a path to the bridge to find four sets of empty tracks.

"It's safe to cross now. I've memorized the train schedules." Jim taps his temple. "It's all up here."

I hope that's not the only thing up there. I'm used to being in control—for better or worse—of my own destiny. Now, I've put all my faith in a homeless man I just met under a bridge. I glance behind me. Still no trains.

"There's a couple of places I frequent on the other side. The food is pretty good."

I assume he raids the dumpsters rather than gets a table inside. I'm having trouble accepting that this is my life now. I flash back to Gomer and Banjo and it helps me feel a little better about my present situation.

"You like Italian?"

If you're talking about eating spaghetti out of a dumpster, I'll have to get back to you.

I'm starving, so I have no choice but to follow this ragamuffin across a dangerous bridge in search of food. He's the closest thing I have to a friend in this new world order. Mitch wouldn't have given someone like Jim the time of day. I feel sorry for Jim, and maybe a little for Mitch.

We reach the other side and descend to street level, a hobo and his hideous little dog walking off the tracks. If I had my wallet, I might buy him some new clothes and get him a shave and haircut. But I guess that's not how this—whatever *this* is—works. Also, I don't have any pockets. In fact, I have nothing. I envy a ratty old homeless guy who lives in a box under a bridge because I don't even have a box of my own.

"Come on, Junior, keep up."

I'm trying. These little legs are useless.

"It's only a few more minutes."

We stay off the main roads. Jim seems to know all the shortcuts. Tutti's Italian Restaurant and the Black Duck share a parking lot. I stop and watch Jim walk toward the Italian place. Mitch usually had some kind of a gastrointestinal event after eating tomato sauce, so I head toward the Duck.

When Jim notices I'm not following, he whistles. "You don't want Italian?"

I shake my head and continue toward the Duck. *I like the Duck. In fact, when I get my hands on my trust fund, I just might buy the place.* Unfortunately, I'm required to finish college to unlock the money. For that to happen, I need to hold a pen or type on a keyboard, neither of which is possible in my present condition. Even with those things, Mitch is presently clinging to a C average in his seventh semester. Of course, that doesn't include the two semesters he partied his way to an incomplete.

Jim shrugs. "Okay. One of the cooks there helps me out sometimes, usually with food that's been sent back or is on its way to the dumpster."

He reaches down and picks me up, which makes me a little uncomfortable.

Is this really necessary?

"He's gonna love you," he says as he tucks me under his arm.

I know what I look like. Is this cook blind? What are we having, see-food surprise?

Jim knocks on a door marked *Employees Only*. A man around Jim's age wearing a white apron answers. He steps outside when he sees us.

"Hey, Jim." He turns to me. "Who you got there?"

"This is my new dog, Junior."

Wait. Your new dog?

"Hey, Junior." Another man is touching me. "Where did you find her?"

"She found me."

"Well, your timing is perfect. I just had some steaks come back. The customer said they were overdone. I've also got a pile of fries I've been saving for you. I'll throw it all together and heat it up. Just give me a minute."

"Did you hear that, Junior? Steak," Jim says as he strokes the top of my head.

You wouldn't believe how well I hear.

Apron man returns and hands Jim a large bag.

"Bless you, my friend. I appreciate your kindness."

It smells like heaven. *Ditto.*

"Sure. Any time." He wags a finger at us. "Be careful out there."

Is this guy for real? I can't believe the compassion I just witnessed. Apron man likely risked his minimum wage job to feed a homeless man and his ugly dog, while someone like Mitch sat out front stuffing his face and drinking overpriced wine with his girl *du jour.*

Jim sets me down. "Wait here." He returns a few moments later, holding up a loaf of Italian bread. "It's a couple of days old, but still good."

I take his word for it. I wouldn't ask where or how he got it even if I could. We hop down to the rocky shoreline that runs under the I-95 bridge.

Jim stops by a large flat rock. "We're here." He sits and sets the bag next to him. "Hop up here, girl."

I stare at the boulder knowing there is no way my tiny legs could catapult me up there. I let out a whine, and he picks me up. *Not a bad view from up here.*

The sun, the water, and the smell of cooked meat remind me of having lunch at that restaurant on the beach in Cancun. Well, almost. Apparently, the bar has been lowered a bit.

He removes two takeout containers from the bag and sets one down in front of me. Instinct takes over as soon as he opens it. French fries scatter as I tear into the meat like a wild animal. Mitch ate steak all the time, usually smothered in mushrooms and onions. However, it's a first for this lifetime, and beyond delicious even without the toppings. After I wolf down the steak, I gobble up the scattered fries and lick my chops.

"You want some bread?"

Mitch would have lectured him on the appropriate time during the meal to serve bread. I grab it from his hand with my teeth. When I finish, I clean up the crumbs from the rock like a vacuum cleaner. I feel like I should apologize for my savage behavior, but I was hungry. And I'm literally an animal.

My stomach is full, but there's always room for dessert.

Jim pulls out another container. "There's more."

Where's dessert? I nudge the bag and two individually wrapped cookies fall out.

"You want dessert? Okay. We'll save this for later."

I pick one up with my teeth and retreat to the corner of the rock. I paw at the wrapper, forgetting how helpless I am. It's not working, and I'm frustrated. I let out an expletive that sounds like a bark.

"Come here. Let me help you."

I don't want anybody's help. You might think I'm being stubborn, but I'm not accustomed to asking for help. I need to do this for myself. With the package in my teeth, I shake my head back and forth with such force that cookie pieces fly in every direction.

Jim looks at me like I'm about to get a lecture. Instead, he asks if I want his cookie.

I don't want your cookie. This isn't about a cookie. It's about my inability to do anything for myself. But you wouldn't understand, would you?

I walk to the edge of the rock and look down. Too far to jump. I bark. *I know I just said I don't want any help, but how about you get me down from here?*

"You want to get down?"

Yes, please.

He deposits me on the ground, and I take off running along the shore. He chases after me. I want to drown my sorrow, and I don't care if it's at the bottom of a bottle or the Saugatuck River. I turn toward the water, but Jim is there to block me.

"The water's too cold to swim."

That's the point, Einstein.

"I'm sorry. I should have opened the cookie for you. Next time—"

I bark. There isn't going to be a next time. I'm going to find whoever did this to me and get my life back.

"No more cookies. Let's go home and take a nap. I've got a nice blanket you can use for a bed."

I consider his offer. If I can't drown myself in the river, a nap sounds like the next best thing.

We gather up the trash, and by we I mean Jim, and stop at the dumpster outside the restaurant. There's a man inside, rooting around in the garbage.

Jim glances at me, then looks at the container in his hand. "If you come out of there, I've got some steak and fries for you."

What are you doing, Jim?

The man looks up from his foraging.

Jim holds up the container. "Here you go, brother."

"Are you sure?"

"Take it. I'm full. No reason you shouldn't be, too."

I stare at Jim and wonder if I'm not looking at Mother Theresa in disguise. He has no idea where his next meal is coming from, but he's willing to give a steak dinner to a random stranger he finds in a dumpster.

I watch in disbelief as the man climbs out, smelling a little worse than Jim, if that's even possible. He takes the food, they exchange a few pleasantries, and he's on his way.

Jim deposits everything but the paper bag into the same dumpster the man just climbed out of. He folds the bag and slips it into his back pocket.

THAT he keeps, because you never know when something like a paper bag might save your life. Poor Jim's got a screw loose under all that hair.

Preoccupied with my hunger on the way to lunch, I hadn't noticed the spaces between the railroad ties through which you can see the water below. I notice this now and freak out. It doesn't seem to be a problem for Jim with his normal-sized human legs.

I hop from one railroad tie to the next. Halfway across the bridge, my back legs slip through an opening. Jim continues to walk, unaware of my predicament.

Hey! A little help here?

I'm wedged between two ties and slipping fast. I dig my front paws into the oily wood. They won't hold me for long. I bark, and Jim turns around. My mind races. I seriously consider letting go. What have I got to look forward to? Living in a box and eating from dumpsters, unable to do anything for myself? I didn't sign up for this, and frankly, I've had about all I can take.

Jim shouts and races toward me. It might be in his best interest to join me at the bottom of the river, but I can't make that decision for him. I haven't let go yet. It's harder than I thought it would be. The uncertainty of what lies beyond that final leap keeps me holding on to life. What if it's worse than my present situation? Not likely, but possible.

Jim arrives and grabs hold of my paws and pulls me to safety. For better or worse, the decision has been made for me. A tear rolls down his cheek as he holds me in his arms like I'm one of his children who ran into the street. I don't know what to do with that.

We walk the rest of the way home, a hobo carrying his hideous little dog along the tracks.

CHAPTER EIGHT

Back in the box, Jim goes through his bags and pulls out a blanket. He clears a space in the corner and lays it down for me. I wonder what else he might have in the rest of those bags. The blanket is clean and soft. I recline, grateful that my belly is full, but still a little shaken from the bridge incident.

I don't want to get too comfortable here and end up like Jim. I'm better than him. This is not my home or my life. I look down at this pathetic dog body. Or my body.

Jim flops down into his chair, and I study him from my corner. What's his story? How did he end up here? Who are these forgotten people living on the fringe of society?

"A penny for your thoughts," Jim says.

I couldn't take your money, and not just because of the pockets thing.

"You're welcome to stay as long as you like. I enjoy the company."

Thanks, Jim. Truth is, I don't know how I would make it on my own, so I'm kind of stuck here until I figure out how to get my old life back.

A long silence descends on the box.

"I haven't always been like this, you know."

I could say the same thing.

"I had a pretty good job on Wall Street."

He has my attention.

"Had a beautiful wife and a condo in the city with a view of the park."

I'm surprised to hear this, but with these big googly eyes, I always look surprised. I sit wheezing and snorting like I'm having an asthma attack and can't find my inhaler. I'm not too worried. Big Dog assured me it was normal for this breed, and I'll get used to it. I'm still waiting.

"I was good at my job picking winners and thought I could do the same at the racetrack and casino. That didn't go so well. Over the course of two years, I lost my house, my wife, and my dignity."

His is your typical riches-to-rags story. My story is similar, but I don't even have any rags. I get a strange urge to walk over to Jim and let him pet me, like somehow that might comfort him. I fight the urge for obvious reasons, but inner Mitch loses another one. Silence descends and I amble over to where he sits.

"I had the world on a string, now I'm dangling at the end of that same string."

Once again, I know the feeling, and we commiserate in silence.

He picks me up and sets me in his lap. "There's a moral to every story," he says as he strokes the length of my back. "Mine is to be grateful for what you have. You can never be happy if you always want more."

Very profound, but do you realize you're talking to a dog? I guess if you include Mitch in the equation, our stories aren't that different, but I'm not feeling grateful. I have nothing.

He smiles at me like I might understand. I don't. I'm having trouble wrapping my head around his situation. It's hard to tell how old he is, probably closing in on fifty. He lives in a cardboard box, with no money and little in the way of worldly possessions, yet he can sit here with a smile on his face like he doesn't have a care in the world. On top of that, he's willing to share what little he has with a stray dog and a dumpster diver.

This man is old enough to be my father, and he's living in a box. I think about Father and wonder what Mitch's life would have been like if he'd been raised by someone with Jim's compassion and generosity. Perhaps those things and Father's level of wealth and privilege are mutually exclusive.

I've never stopped to ask such questions before, but I see the world differently through a dog's eyes. I haven't decided if it's better or worse, just different.

It's surprisingly comfortable in Jim's lap, and I... *Oh, God.* He scratches my ears again, which I've just decided is my favorite thing. I close my eyes and eventually drift off to sleep.

I awake some time later feeling embarrassed, so I scamper off to my blanket and fall asleep again.

"Hey, Junior."

I open my eyes.

"We're going for another walk."

Reluctantly, I stand.

"We have to go pick up tomorrow's breakfast. The donut shop at the train station closes at six, and they throw away anything that hasn't sold."

This guy's a genius. I'm hungry. You think we can get a head start on breakfast tonight?

We have to cross the bridge again. Apparently, there's nothing of interest on this side of the river, so I need to get used to it. Jim offers to carry me. I'm nervous. I'll get over my fear eventually, but I let him carry me this time.

They're locking up the donut shop when we arrive, so we stroll around back to pick up our order. One garbage bag full of donuts to go. Jim pulls the bag from the top of the dumpster pile and opens it.

He looks inside and smiles. "We have a good selection tonight, but no chocolate for you."

I can identify each one by smell. My mouth is watering.

He pulls the big paper bag from his pocket and fills it up. I bark, and he tosses a glazed donut in my direction. It's gone in two bites, and I give him the sad eyes like I want another. It works. He tosses me a fritter.

"We need to save some for breakfast. Besides, you don't want to spoil your dinner."

Dinner?

"We're having fresh fish tonight. Catch of the day."

There are plenty of seafood places around, but if we're going out to dinner, we both need a shower first.

"I've collected some fishing gear and taught myself how to fish."

I'm guessing we can forget about the showers.

I make it back across the bridge without being carried and consider it quite an accomplishment. I couldn't let Jim carry me again. He might drop the donuts.

Back home, Jim retrieves a makeshift fishing pole from behind the box. Clearly not something you buy at a sporting goods store, it consists of a tree branch, some string that may or may not have been actual fishing line, and a real fishhook.

I'd never been fishing, so when he pulls a foot-long fish out of the river after only a few minutes, I'm impressed. It flops around on the rocky shore, and I take a step back. I don't have a clue what kind it is. They all look alike to me, but Jim says it's good eatin'.

He skins and guts it with his pocketknife, then retrieves a bag of kindling from inside the box. Another mystery is solved about the contents of his bags. Then we play a lazy man's game of fetch where I retrieve sticks he hasn't thrown. In Jim's defense, he retrieves a few as well.

He cooks the fish over an open fire as dusk surrounds us. Mitch loved seafood, but since I slipped on this dog suit, I'm not a big fan. However, hunger makes everything taste better.

We eat right here on the shore while the crackling flames cast flickering shadows on our faces.

"You know, Junior," Jim says, his voice tinged with a hint of nostalgia or maybe regret, "I used to have it all—a successful career, a family..."

Now the truth comes out. The happy hobo isn't so happy. How could he be?

"I spent too much time chasing the wrong things."

Wait. If money and a condo in the city are the wrong things, I don't want to be right.

"I wish I could turn back time, make different choices."

You and me both, brother. You don't happen to have a time machine stashed behind your box with the fishing equipment, do you? Stupid question. If he did, I'd be sitting here alone, starving to death.

A voice somewhere in my head tells me Jim and I aren't that different. At first this sounds ridiculous, but I guess I had it all, too. Yes, but I didn't gamble it away. It's possible I'd consumed a little too much alcohol that night, but it was Ashley's fault. *There you go again, blaming your problems on everyone else*, the voice says. I have two words to say to that. *Shut up!*

In a quiet moment under the stars, my canine compassion trumps everything, and I move closer to offer some silent assurance to Jim that he's a good man and things will get better. I'm not sure I believe it, but it's what any dog in my position would do. We sit in silence as he strokes my back. It feels good to have someone to talk to, even if he can't understand me. Perhaps Jim is thinking the same thing.

Eventually, Jim stands and kicks some sand on the last of the glowing embers. "Come on, Junior, let's get some sleep. We've got work to do tomorrow."

Work?

In the morning, we go on what Jim refers to as a scavenger hunt, which sounds better than "collecting empty bottles and cans for the nickel deposit." He says the money helps with his living expenses, whatever that means. He's not spending it on soap or breath mints.

Looking past the obvious, Jim is decent company, and I'm grateful for the food and shelter he provides, not to mention he saved my life. But I want more, and I don't understand why he doesn't.

As the days wear on, I can't help thinking Jim is wasting his life. He's a smart guy who worked on Wall Street, probably making six figures. So, he made a mistake. We've both made mistakes, but he is still Jim, the human. Unlike Mitch, the dog, he has a chance to turn things around. He appears content with his meager existence, but it can't possibly be the way he really feels.

I think I know how I can help him, but I'm not ready to leave yet. Where would I go?

CHAPTER NINE

I'm up half the night tossing and turning in the throes of a moral dilemma, something Mitch had never dealt with. The other voice in my head is telling me what to do. *Help him out*, it says. *He can help himself, if he wants to*, I reply. *It's every man—and dog—for himself.*

Eventually this other voice, the *dog voice,* I call it, wears me down. Jim saved my life and helped me out when I needed it. I guess I can return the favor. The first step is to get him out from under this bridge. Not something I can do alone.

My first thought is the police. I can't just pick up a phone and call them, so I need to get creative. Where can I find a police officer around here? The donut shop comes to mind. Everyone jokes about cops and donuts, but I'm pretty sure it's at least half true.

We return from lunch and a scavenger hunt on an overcast Saturday afternoon. The air is cool for mid-May, and the threat of rain has cut our foraging short. With nothing else to do, Jim curls up on his mattress, and I watch him from my blanket in the corner. As much as I'd like to join him in dreamland, I have a mission—Operation Save Jim From Himself. The name's too long, so I shorten it to Operation Save Jim.

I sneak outside and walk to the donut shop. No cops, so I find a spot to wait. Dogs can sit for hours with no effort because they live in the here and now. Humans are more interested in the future. However, that only holds true until dinnertime. I remember Jim saying the shop closes at six.

I don't have a watch or phone, so I don't know what time it is when the police cruiser pulls up. Two officers, a man and a woman, enter the shop. As I wait outside, a debate rages in my mind whether I should have approached them before they went inside.

It must be the Mitch in me, but I'm impatient. What are they doing in there? Is the selection so big they can't decide? Did they sit down to have a cup of coffee and some leisurely conversation? Is this some kind of office—or in this case, officer—romance? I bark a couple of times to relieve my frustration. Surprisingly, it helps.

When they finally exit the building, I approach. Without a speaking voice, all I can do is bark. The woman notices me first and approaches. Mitch had a thing for chicks in uniform.

"What's the matter, girl? Are you lost?" She scans the parking lot.

We haven't had time to work out a system—one bark for yes, two for no. I bark twice anyway. Perhaps it's universal. I want to lead them to Jim, so I steal a scene from a movie Mitch watched as a child. I turn and run a few feet, then stop and look at them. *You need to follow me.* I repeat the run-and-bark routine a couple more times, hoping she gets the message.

In the meantime, the other one approaches. "Looks like she wants to show us something."

Good, you've seen that one, too. I bark.

"Let's see what it is."

Perfect. Follow me. I turn and run. After twenty feet, I stop to check on them. They're following. I slow my pace so I don't lose them. The donuts are obviously affecting their running ability.

They follow me to the bridge, then stop. I turn and bark when I realize they're not following me across. Nothing. They look confused as they talk between themselves.

"Come back here," the cute one calls. "It's too dangerous."

You're preaching to the choir, honey, but I don't know any other way to get across. I hesitate, considering my options.

"We're going to lose her," she says to her partner. "I'll follow. You take the car and meet us on the other side."

"Seriously, Claire? It's a dog."

She starts across.

Her partner shrugs. "Be careful," he calls, then turns and runs.

I wait for Claire on the other side, then lead her down under the bridge.

"This better be worth it," she says from a few feet behind me.

She stops when she sees the box. I wait while she radios her partner, then drops to one knee beside me. She smells nice.

"Is there someone inside there?" she whispers.

I bark once.

"Junior," Jim calls from inside.

Claire places her hand on her gun.

Relax, sister. It's not Osama bin Laden in there.

Her partner joins us, and they exchange a series of hand signals.

I'm beginning to have mixed feelings about this. I believe I'm helping Jim but don't expect him to see it that way.

Jim appears in the doorway. "Hey, Junior. Where have you been?" He notices the police officers behind me and his face explodes with fear and surprise. "Junior! What have you done?"

I'm not sure. I think I'm helping you.

"Sir, please step outside," the partner says.

Jim glares at me. "I should have named you Judas." He disappears inside.

The accuracy of his biblical reference stings, and I wonder if I made the right choice. *Come on, Jim, you live in a cardboard box. Puppies live in boxes, not people. You deserve better than this.*

Both officers draw their weapons. "Please step outside."

Don't hurt him. I have second thoughts about involving the police and their guns.

"We just want to talk."

Jim reappears in the doorway.

"Show us your hands."

Is this really necessary? He's unarmed. Then I remember the bat.

Jim raises his hands, and Claire and her partner holster their weapons.

They interrogate him and explain that he can't live under the bridge. They promise him a hot meal and a warm bed at a shelter.

Claire whispers to her partner. "What do we do with the dog?"

Like I'm not going to hear. Dogs hear everything. One of the few perks.

He checks his watch. "Animal Control is closed."

Good. I'm not going back there.

Claire looks at me, and I give her the sad eyes.

"This might go easier if we let him bring his dog. Maybe the shelter will keep him over the weekend. We can deal with her on Monday."

Deal with me? What's that supposed to mean?

Chapter Ten

The volunteer who is doing the intake at the shelter says no dogs. Jim is still looking at me like I'm a traitor, so I don't think he cares. Claire pleads her case, but the volunteer is not in a position to make exceptions to the rules, so she asks to speak to the person in charge.

Staying at the shelter with Jim feels like a better option than whatever they might have in mind for Plan B. Once again, I have no control over my own destiny.

Sarah Turner, the shelter manager, joins us, and Claire explains our situation. Before she agrees to anything, Sarah looks me over, then extends her hand. It smells like peanuts. I'm not accustomed to licking other people's hands, but in this case, I make an exception. It's still a little awkward having people pick me up, but I don't resist when she lifts me off the ground.

Don't be fooled by appearances. I'm not really a dog. I'm Mitch Westcott. Perhaps you've heard of the Westcotts.

"There's not much else we can do with her until Animal Control opens on Monday," Claire says.

"I see." She strokes my back. "We've made exceptions in the past for service dogs. I could probably bend the rules this one time."

"It's just for the weekend. I can come by on Monday and get her."

I give Sarah the sad eyes. She holds out her peanut hand, and I lick it again.

"I think we can accommodate her until then." She holds me up to her face and speaks to me like I'm an infant. "You're gonna be a good girl, aren't you?"

If you only knew who you were talking to. I don't know how to respond. I try to nod my head and a couple of snorts slip out.

Everyone laughs. Except Jim.

The cops leave, and I sit and watch the volunteer who said I couldn't stay, complete Jim's intake. I don't think he's a hater, just a minion doing his job. When they're finished, we join the other residents in the dining room. It's almost dinnertime, and I'm feeling it.

They are a noisy bunch, laughing and telling stories as we wait for our meal. I'm not laughing, and I can't understand why they are. Sam—these guys don't like to use last names—has kitchen duty tonight, and word is he's had some experience cooking in the military. Twice a week, Sam gives the volunteers a break and prepares dinner. He doesn't disappoint tonight.

I don't get a place setting, but I eat well, being fed by many hands under the table. Jim's isn't one of them. His cold shoulder is getting colder.

After dinner, I follow him to his room. He shuts the door in my face before I can step inside.

Not cool! He'll come around after a few nights in a proper bed. *Speaking of beds, where's mine?* I look around. Okay, I guess I'll sleep in the hall.

I curl up on the carpet across from Jim's door. I've noticed dogs sleep more than people, so I don't fight the urge to close my eyes. Some time later, I'm awakened by the minion. Apparently, sleeping in the hall is not allowed. Fire regulations or something. He sure likes to follow rules. Mitch would have slipped him a twenty-dollar bill, but, well, the pockets thing again. I wander downstairs to find three of the residents watching a baseball game on TV in the living room. I pick out a spot next to the sofa and join them. This sure beats living in a box without a TV.

The room is full of Yankees fans, myself included. Mitch made the forty-five-mile trip to Yankee Stadium many times, including game six of the 2009 World Series. The guys in the room seem like a surprisingly tight-knit group of fans for living in temporary housing, but sports will do that to you. I want to fit in. After a few well-timed barks and snorts, Rocco, who appears to be their unofficial leader, pats the cushion next to himself on the couch. I struggle with these short legs, so he helps me up. He introduces me to Mickey and Boner, and we settle in for the rest of the game.

My attention is split between the game and this trio of misfits. Rocco is the alpha dog, the brains—and brawn—of the outfit. His shirtsleeves strain against his beefy, tattooed arms. Mickey is the sidekick. He's a nervous little guy who can't sit still and adds the comic relief to Rocco's no-nonsense style. Boner is a bit of a mystery. He's not the sharpest knife in the drawer, asking dumb questions and making pointless comments. He's the kind of guy everyone loves and feels sorry for at the same time.

Most of these guys are pretty rough around the edges, not Mitch's kind of crowd, so they don't mind hanging around with a goofy-looking dog like me. *Move over all you poodles and doodles, Pugzilla is in the house.*

Rocco reaches over every now and again to pat my head or scratch behind my ear. When the Yanks win in the bottom of the ninth on a walk-off home run, Rocco holds up my paw so the guys can high-five me. I bark, and snort, and think I need to stay here, at least until the end of the baseball season.

All the hootin' and hollerin' brings Jim to the living room door. He lingers for a moment before moving on. Just before lights out, Rocco produces a thick blanket for my bed and gives me a pat on the head to say goodnight. I get the feeling he's really a big teddy bear in disguise.

In the morning, I realize there's an upside to my inability to speak. When you don't spend all your time thinking about what you're going to say next, you have a lot of time to listen. Everyone has something to say at breakfast, including Jim. They all seem like decent guys who have made some bad decisions or fallen on hard times, most through no fault of their own. Except for Larry. He's a troublemaker.

It's Sunday, so the house is full. During the week, most of the guys look for work, do odd jobs, or use the computers at the library. Currently, nineteen souls call this place home. It's like the *Island of Misfit Toys*, a place where broken toys were sent on a Christmas show Mitch watched as a kid.

However, unlike the toys, they're not stuck here forever. It's a steppingstone on the way to rebuild their lives. With the help of Sarah and people at other local agencies, they find work and subsidized housing. Many are grateful and return as volunteers, helping others to succeed.

This is a side of life Mitch has never seen. It's eye-opening.

While my inner dog voice urges me to somehow help these poor souls, my inner Mitch stresses the importance of first helping myself. As the battle rages on in my head, I wonder what a dog can do that might make a difference. Ashley would know. She always helped others, something Mitch discouraged because it meant less time spent with him.

As we all know, the world revolved around Mitchell Patrick Westcott III.

Chapter Eleven

After breakfast, I find a sunny spot in the yard and fall asleep. When I awake, I wander into the house to find a crowd in the living room. The Yankees are playing a day game, and Rocco has saved me a seat. I feel like one of the guys.

Jim is there, and I sense his stare. He looks away and pretends to watch the game when I glance at him, but he doesn't fool me. I think he likes it here and regrets the way he's treated me since we arrived. Part of me wants to stick it to him and tell him he blew it. But, besides the fact that I can't speak, a bigger part of me wants to let him off the hook. It must be a dog thing.

Since I've become a dog, my senses have improved significantly. In addition to hearing and smell, I can sense what people are feeling. It's exhausting sometimes, especially in a place like this. I try to shield myself from the drama, but that's not how dogs roll.

It's only my second day here, and I feel like I might want to stay for a while. The food is good, I've made some new friends, and I feel a camaraderie Mitch never felt. His wealth, and perhaps his ego, separated him from the common man. Ego is something dogs don't possess. And without pockets, or thumbs to write a check, money does me no good.

My friend, Officer Claire, calls on Monday to tell Sarah that Animal Control is overcrowded and can't take me. I'm relieved. Sarah breaks the news to the guys that I'll be staying until at least the end of the week. Everyone cheers, including Jim.

I'm something of a celebrity at the house, and I strut around like the big dog on campus. There's talk of designating me the unofficial mascot of the Franklin Street Homeless Shelter. All the guys want to hang with me. I guess there's some sort of vibe dogs give off that soothes the human soul. Mitch was unaware, as he was about most matters of the heart.

I'm not saying Mitch was a bad guy. He had his moments. Some people are just wired differently. I think a lot of it has to do with the way they're raised. Unfortunately, we can't all be dogs. The world would be a better place, but who'd pay the bills and pick up our poop?

On Tuesday, a few of the guys take me out into the yard and surprise me with a can of tennis balls Mickey bought at Walmart. He pops it open and throws the first ball across the yard. I know what he wants. He wants me to chase it down and bring it back to him. Fat chance. *Wait. Who am I kidding?* It looks like fun, and I take off after it.

Unlike humans, dogs can enjoy mundane, repetitive tasks indefinitely with pure joy. The guys take turns throwing the balls. My tongue hangs out, and I snort like a locomotive as I chase them all over the yard. In my mind, I'm Secretariat in the last leg of the Triple Crown. In reality, I'm more like a drunken pirate with a wooden leg. We're all having fun, so who cares?

George, the oldest of the group, watches from a chair in the yard. He keeps to himself and looks sad most of the time. When the guys try to talk to him, he chases them away with his cane. He sits alone and coughs up a lung now and then. After a half hour of fetching little yellow balls, I sit next to him, wheezing almost as much as he is. He doesn't chase me away.

I look up at George and study the lines on his face. They tell me he's had a rough life. He must feel my stare because he turns to me. We lock eyes, his expression unreadable. Then he smiles. It's a small one and it flashes quickly, but I see it. This dog vibe is powerful.

After dinner, Sarah gets the group together to tell them how she feels about having a dog in the house. While I consider myself a valued member of the community, I can't be sure the boss feels the same way. Given what she's witnessed over the past few days, she thinks I'm good for morale and offers to make some calls to keep me around... on one condition.

"Junior is not a proper name for a female dog, so we're going to have a vote to choose a new one."

She gives them twenty-four hours to come up with a more appropriate moniker.

After the meeting, many of us retire to the living room for our nightly ritual of watching syndicated sitcom re-runs. I don't mind the name Junior, but knowing it's shorthand for Punch Jr. makes me feel like it might be time for a change. I'm not fully on board with the whole female thing yet, but I put my trust in this bunch of rough riders to come up with a name that isn't too feminine.

They throw around names and lobby for their favorite. I hear Riley, Bailey, and Murphy. All solid names. I'm okay with any one of them.

Then, one of the ugliest dogs I've ever seen, present company excluded, appears on the TV screen. She belongs to a character named Jay Pritchett, and her name is Stella. I cringe, hoping no one is paying attention. Immediately, everyone notices the resemblance and "Stella" becomes the front-runner for my new name.

Twenty-three hours later, sitting in a room with a group of men who I thought were my friends, my name is Stella. I don't like it, but it won by a landslide. Once again, humans control my destiny. Larry voted for *Pugly*, so I guess it could have been worse.

I need a stiff drink, but like just about everything else I think I want, it's not going to happen. I'm tired and I need to be alone. My bed is in the living room, so I wander upstairs. Halfway down the hall, I hear George cough up a lung. This guy has a real problem. The only upside is that he has a private room because no one can sleep through all the noises he makes.

His door is open a crack, and I push it with my head. I can't see him, but I hear him rustling around in bed. It's early, and I wonder if he's okay. Of course, I'm unable to ask, so I amble over to the side of the bed.

"Who's there?" he whispers between coughs.

I smell fear. I'm concerned and let out a whimper.

"Is that you, Junior?"

I wish. It's Stella now, but you can call me whatever you like.

His bed is low, but not low enough for me to hop up there. Dogs are tenacious, so I find a way. The boxes at the foot of the bed act as stairs, and I climb up next to him on the bed and turn up the dog vibe. I don't have to tell you it feels weird climbing into bed with another man. I shake it off and lie at his feet. They stink, but I shake that off, too.

"You're a good girl."

I can't see it, but I feel his smile. *Yeah, I guess I am.*

Chapter Twelve

The next morning, I awake disoriented after spending the night at the foot of George's bed. I didn't sleep well. Jim used to complain about my snoring when we lived in the box. I doubt George even heard me over the racket coming from his end of the bed.

I'm tired and spend much of the day napping in the living room. When I'm not catching up on my beauty rest, I make the rounds to ensure everything is running smoothly. With all the knuckleheads that pass through here, Sarah can use all the help she can get.

Most of the guys enjoy my company and talk to me like a friend and confidant. It's as satisfying as it is eye-opening. Their secrets are safe with me. I couldn't tell anyone even if I wanted to. Perhaps I'll write a book in my next life... if I have thumbs.

After dinner, there's a kerfuffle and tempers flare. A new guy, Alex, claims money is missing from his room, and he wants it back. Of course, everyone denies involvement in the theft. His roommate becomes the prime suspect, but he was out all day. Some accuse Alex of making up the story to get attention. I sense he's telling the truth. The group eventually disperses without a resolution.

The guys are on edge the following day. I count myself among them, but for a different reason. It's the end of the week, and Claire is on her way over to pick me up. I know this because I spend some time each day in Sarah's office, eavesdropping on her conversations. I have the perfect cover. Dogs don't understand human conversation. Or do they?

I thought I had more time. As soon as I hear she's coming for me, I panic and run. I can't decide whether to leave the building or stay and hide. Leaving is probably the safer option, but where do I go? I don't even have a box to live in anymore. Besides, I like it here. I choose the latter and look for a place to hide.

I run into the living room, where a few of the guys are watching TV, and shimmy under the couch. No good. My wheezing will give me away if Claire is in the room. I need help, but I have no way of asking for it. What I wouldn't give to have my voice back. My mind spins through possible scenarios, none of them good, as Sarah walks in. I wiggle my way to the edge for a better view.

"Has anyone seen Stella?"

"She's under the couch," Larry says.

I stay put as Larry suffers the angry glares of the others in the room.

"The police are on their way here to pick her up."

The guys moan and groan and express their dismay. Larry tries to hide a smile.

"I can't tell you what to do," Sarah continues, "but perhaps if they think Stella has left us, they'll drop the matter, and we can keep her here."

"This isn't an animal shelter."

More glares. "Shut up, Larry."

"I'm going back to my office before I see Stella. I don't want to lie when I tell them I haven't seen her."

"We'll find a good hiding place," Mickey says.

"I didn't hear that," Sarah calls over her shoulder as she walks away.

Rocco stands. "Larry and I are going for a long walk."

Larry hunkers down in his chair. "The hell we are."

Everyone else in the room stands and surrounds Larry's chair.

Rocco crosses his beefy arms in front of his chest. "We can do this the easy way or the hard way. Your choice."

After Larry reluctantly leaves the house with Rocco, the others scramble to find a suitable hiding place for yours truly. The plan is to hide me in some forgotten corner of the building and convince the authorities that I've left, with no forwarding address.

They lead me up to a storage room on the third floor. It's stuffy and a little creepy, like an attic. They assure me no one will look for me up there and shut the door.

Don't forget about me!

I don't like it up here, but I have no choice if I want to stay at the shelter. I wander around, sniffing everything. The floor creaks, and I can't tell if I'm hearing my own footsteps or I'm not alone up here. The latter creeps me out, so I investigate. The room is empty, but I find a loose floorboard in one corner. I don't have thumbs, so I look for something I can use to pry it up.

When I return with a coat hanger in my teeth, I realize this is going to be harder than I'd imagined. I feel there's something sinister about this situation, so I use my paws and teeth to wedge the hook between the boards. The plan is to use the hanger as a lever to pry out the loose board. I'm proud of myself until the hanger slips out when I push on the opposite end. I'm not discouraged and try it again, but the result is the same.

The third time is the charm, and the edge of the floorboard pops up enough to push it out of the way. In the space between the floor and the ceiling below is a stash of what appears to be ill-gotten booty.

After the recent theft, I'd overheard a couple of guys talk about a cellphone and watch that went missing a couple of weeks ago. They searched all the rooms but found nothing.

Whoever it was, and I have a pretty good idea, was able to avoid detection by stashing the loot up here.

It's dark under the floor, but I can make out a couple of cellphones, a watch, a pile of cash, and some drugs. Who's going to report their illegal drugs missing, right?

The thief is still here, or he would have taken his booty with him. I'm unable to tell anyone, so I need to do something. I could make a fuss when they come to get me—IF they come to get me—hoping they'll follow me to the stash. But if I do, everyone will just deny any knowledge of the crime.

No, we need to catch the perp in the act. I push the floorboard back into place and hide the hanger. I need to stake out the third floor and confront the perp. Better yet, I'll get Rocco to confront him. I don't know how, but I'll figure something out.

I'm tired from all this detective work, so I curl up by the door and drift off to sleep. Some time later, the creaking of the door wakes me.

Mickey drops to one knee. "Hey, Stella. It's over. You're a free man, er, dog." He strokes my back. "We convinced the cops you were gone, probably halfway to Norwalk by now. They'll probably stop looking for you."

I bark my appreciation and consider myself a lucky dog.

Later, when I wander into the dining room for dinner, conversation stops, and I sense something's up. Mickey calls me over from the end of the table.

Okay, I'll play along.

Then I see it. A shiny new bowl with my name on it, sitting in the corner of the room. I don't care for the name, but I love the bowl. *Thanks, guys.*

I amble over, give it a couple of sniffs, and turn toward the table. Everyone but Larry cheers like Aaron Judge hit another one out of the park. I'm touched. No one has ever been this nice to me.

"It's official," Rocco says. "You're one of us now."

I couldn't have a bigger lump in my throat if I'd swallowed a tennis ball. Imagine that. Mitchell Patrick Westcott III having dinner with his homeless family... and Larry.

CHAPTER THIRTEEN

The house is full on Saturday morning. During the week, the guys who have jobs leave the house early, but today everyone is here. The mood is upbeat as they talk about how they tricked the cops and welcomed me into their group.

Larry is uncharacteristically friendly and goes out of his way to talk to me and stroke my back. He produces a piece of bacon he'd saved from breakfast. I love bacon, but it feels like a bribe. He's up to something. I eat it anyway.

"You dodged a bullet yesterday," he says. "I'm glad you'll be staying with us."

Bullshit!

He'd heard about my time in the attic yesterday and is afraid I stumbled across his stash. Perhaps I didn't cover my tracks well enough. At any rate, this is no coincidence. A chameleon doesn't change its color for no reason.

My suspicions are confirmed. Larry is our thief. And I'll do whatever I can to expose him. But if he knows I know, he might try to eliminate the threat. I need to watch my back. *Yikes!* The bacon. What if it was poisoned? I need to stick my finger down my throat and bring it up. Wait... I don't have fingers. I better go lie down so I can die in my sleep.

I open my eyes a couple of hours later and see my paws, so I'm still a dog. The room looks like the same one where I fell asleep. I'm not sure why I'm glad to be alive, but I am. Better the devil you know than the devil you don't, I guess.

Okay. Maybe I overreacted. I have to laugh at myself for thinking I ate poisoned bacon. I'm still going to watch my back.

***

I meet Jennifer for the first time on Monday. She's a social worker who visits once a week from Fairfield to help these guys battle their demons and make a fresh start. I'm interested to find out what goes on in these sessions, so I follow Mickey into her office. I have demons of my own and wonder if I might benefit from her counsel.

"Who is this?" Jennifer asks.

"Oh, that's Stella. She lives here now. She's something of a mascot for the house. Everybody loves her."

Yeah, everybody except Larry.

"Do you mind if she stays?" Mickey asks. "I don't know what it is, but I feel calmer when she's around."

"Dogs can have that effect on people."

I notice it, too. During his session, he isn't as nervous and jerky as I've seen him around the house.

As their conversation drones on, my eyes get heavy. I must have fallen asleep, because the next thing I remember is being startled by a loud noise. Mickey is standing next to an overturned chair when I open my eyes.

"You're in denial, Mickey," Jennifer says. "The only way to get through this is to accept the hand you've been dealt and make the best of it. Do the work and get back in the game."

Easy for her to say. I walk over to him, and he picks me up.

"I know you can do this. We're not given anything we can't handle."

Mickey takes a deep breath, rights the fallen chair with his free hand, and sits.

After Mickey's session, Jim walks in. I decide to stick around. After some backstory, he tells her I forced him to take a good look at his life and try to turn things around.

Jennifer smiles. "Sounds like it was no coincidence Stella found you under that bridge."

"I can't disagree. I only wish I hadn't turned my back on her after she ratted me out."

"Your choice of words makes me think you still harbor ill feelings."

"No. I didn't mean it like that. This is the best thing that could have happened. I'm getting the help I need to get back on my feet again."

"Did you tell her?"

Jim frowns as he pauses for a moment. "You realize she's a dog."

"I'm aware. Dogs have feelings, too."

I whimper when he looks at me. I can't help it, it just slips out like I no longer have control of my emotions. Mitch had perfected the art of emotional control, but as time goes by, it seems my human instincts are giving way to something softer, more canine.

Jim pats his leg, and I go to him without hesitation. He picks me up and sets me in his lap. "Sorry, girl, for the way I treated you. Frankly, I didn't like how it all went down, but I see now it was the only way for me to come to terms with the fact that I was wasting my life, and I'm forever grateful for what you did."

I appreciate that, Jim. We're cool.

My tail wants to wag, but it's so tightly curled, it's more of a twitch. I've noticed it has three speeds. There's the vibration, the twitch, and the wag, which isn't much of a wag given the tail's size and shape. Sometimes, I need to wiggle my butt to produce a full-on wag.

"Okay. Now we need to find you a job." Jennifer looks at her notes. "I understand you used to work in finance."

"I did, but I need something new."

"You may need to start at the bottom."

"I understand."

"Good. That will make our search a little easier."

I'm proud of my boy, Jim, and have a good feeling about his future.

After Jim's session, Jennifer shows me some love. She says I have a knack for this kind of work and I'm welcome to attend her sessions anytime.

I beam like a first-grader who has just received a gold star. For the first time in either of my lives, I feel like I'm having a positive impact on others. It's intoxicating, and I want to do more. I can't think of anyone's life that has been made better by Mitch and his narcissism. Have you ever heard of a narcissistic dog? I didn't think so.

I didn't realize chicks went for ugly dogs. She probably feels sorry for me, but I'll take the scratching and petting any way I can get it.

Chapter Fourteen

When I return to the general population, I don't see George. He's too feeble to go out anywhere except to sit in the yard, but it's raining today. I wander upstairs to check on him and hear him in his room coughing up a lung. Maybe both of them. His door is ajar, and I push my way in.

"Can't breathe," he whispers when he sees me.

Yikes! There's nothing I can do but go for help. I run downstairs and bark my stupid head off. I try the follow-me trick, and it works. Rocco is the first on the scene. He helps George sit up in his bed.

Rocco shouts, "Call 9-1-1."

Mickey opens a window to let some fresh air into the stale room. Sam says help is on the way.

I watch from the corner of the room where I can stay out of everyone's way. A whimper slips out. *Hang in there, George.*

I hear a distant siren through the open window. Sam runs downstairs as the sound gets louder. In a matter of minutes, two EMTs charge in and clear the room. I go unnoticed in the corner.

They strap an oxygen mask over George's face and check his vitals. I sense their unspoken apprehension as they bring a gurney in from the hall and transfer poor George from the bed. And, just like that, they're gone. The receding wail of the siren sends chills down my back.

No news the rest of the day about our fallen comrade. George had been somewhat ornery and standoffish, but I could see right through his unpleasant facade. He was hurting both physically and mentally. I don't know the details, but it's obvious his long life had not been filled with sunshine and rainbows. Perhaps he knew the end was near, and he didn't want anyone to get too close.

After a rather somber breakfast, Rocco offers to go down to the hospital and check on George. The news he returns with is not good. George had spent the night in the ICU and might be there for a while. I want to go sit with him and offer some of those good dog vibes, but that's not going to happen.

I wander upstairs and find George's door ajar. I push my way in and sniff around. A heavy sadness hangs in the air like a wet blanket, causing me to wheeze more than usual, but I stay. I tell myself he's coming back.

I'm exhausted and crawl under the bed to escape the heaviness and wait for his return. My silent vigil is short-lived as my head becomes too heavy to hold up. I rest it on my paws and drift off to sleep.

I'm awakened by a creaking floorboard.

George? Yikes, how long have I slept? But it's not George. It's Larry. I hunker down out of sight and hold my breath for fear my wheezing might give me away. There's no reason for him to be in here. No *good* reason, that is.

He creeps around like a thief in the night and stops in front of George's dresser. "I guess you won't be needing this anymore," Larry says as he pockets something shiny from the top drawer.

I want to charge at him and take a bite out of his leg, maybe both of them, but I still possess some ability to reason like a human, so I hold my ground. After he rifles through the rest of George's drawers, Larry turns and stares at the bed. If he looks under here, I'll have no choice but to attack.

Fortunately, for both of us, Larry slithers out of the room, avoiding any confrontation. I hadn't been able to warn the other guys of my suspicion. Now that I've caught him in the act, how can I prove it? I wish I still had my six-foot human body and my voice... and, of course, my pockets.

I creep to the doorway and look down the hall to see Larry climb the stairs to the third floor.

Got you now! I sneak down the hall in the other direction. When I reach the stairs, I descend so quickly I tumble down the last three steps. I right myself and get my bearings as

Rocco approaches. I bark a few times and climb a couple of stairs. *Hurry!* I bark again and run up the stairs.

Rocco motions to Mickey and Boner, and they follow.

I head for the stairway to the third floor with the cavalry close behind. We need to sneak up on Larry and catch him red-handed, so I stop at the bottom of the stairs.

"What's the matter, girl?"

Unfortunately, I don't have an answer they would understand.

"Do you want us to go upstairs?"

"Shhh," Mickey says with a finger to his lips.

Everyone stands still and listens. I hold my breath to prevent any wheezing.

"Someone is up there," Rocco whispers.

It's Larry the Loser. That's what I've been trying to tell you. He's up to no good.

We begin our ascent quietly, with Rocco leading the way. He uses military-style hand signals to communicate with the others, like the commander of the SEAL team closing in on bin Laden.

Larry is on his knees in the corner, working on the floorboard. It pops open and he reaches into his pocket.

"What you doin' up here, Larry?" Rocco says, his voice dripping with accusation.

Larry's head snaps around and his eyes widen, but he makes a quick recovery. "None of your business."

"Looks like you got something in your hand," Mickey says.

"What part of none of your business do you not understand?"

Rocco grabs Larry's wrist and squeezes until his hand opens and a gold watch falls to the floor.

"That's George's watch," Mickey says.

Busted! I walk over to the hole in the floor and bark.

"Is that what I think it is?"

I bark again, and Boner peers into the hole in the floor.

I follow Rocco, Mickey, and Boner as they escort Larry the Loser to his room and wait while he packs his stuff.

I watch with satisfaction.

"They never should have let that stupid dog stay here."

"Shut up and pack."

Yeah. Shut up, loser.

Larry slings a bag over his shoulder, and we follow him to the front door. I enjoy this until we get outside and Larry points a finger at me. "This is your fault, you stupid little mutt."

"Shut up and keep moving."

"You better watch your back," he calls over his shoulder. "I'm comin' for you."

If I were alone, I'd be shaking, but I've got my SEAL team with me.

Chapter Fifteen

The rest of the week is uneventful. In fact, it's refreshing not to have to listen to Larry's wiseass remarks. But his threats still echo in my ears and rattle my nerves.

It's Monday, and Jennifer is here for her weekly visit. She says I'm welcome to attend any or all of the sessions, and I find an appropriate spot beside her chair. I think the guys find my presence comforting, and I'm happy to be there for them. I think a dog's purpose is to be a faithful companion to humans and offer them unconditional love. After living a life where such things held little sway, I find this canine perspective refreshing, but difficult to fully embrace.

Just before lunch, Sarah enters with a grim expression. "I need your help."

"Sure. What's on your mind?"

"I just got a call. There's been a complaint about Stella living here."

A complaint? A dozen centipedes with icy feet crawl up my spine. *Larry!*

"I initially allowed her to stay for a weekend, just until Animal Control opened on Monday. The residents really took to her, and I looked the other way when they came up with a plan to keep her."

"I've enjoyed having her sit in on my sessions." Jennifer smiles. "Her presence puts many of the residents at ease."

"They've made exceptions in the past for service dogs."

Jennifer shakes her head. "Service dogs are trained and certified."

"I was afraid you were going to say that." Her shoulders slump. "They'll force her to leave, and there's nothing I can do about it."

No. Don't make me leave. We can come up with another plan.

"Stella is special," Jennifer says.

I like it so far.

"She's wonderful with the residents." Sarah's eyes widen. "Couldn't you see her working as an emotional support animal?"

Wait, what? Working? What else you got?

"They don't require as much training, do they?"

Jennifer is shaking her head again. "No, but in the State of Connecticut, emotional support animals need to be prescribed by a mental health professional for someone with an actual disability."

"I see." Sarah pauses. "She deserves a good home and loving family."

"I might be able to help with that."

Now we're getting somewhere.

"I have a friend at the Second Chance Pet Adoption Center in Fairfield. She's very good at finding the right homes for animals like Stella."

Animals like Stella? What's that supposed to mean?

"In fact, they're preparing for their annual Pet Adoption Expo. It takes place next weekend in the park. It's a big deal. They re-home a lot of animals."

"Sounds perfect."

"I'll give her a call."

I try to keep an open mind. I don't want to leave my friends, but they'll all move on eventually. The Adoption Expo sounds promising, but I want to have a say in who I go home with. I know that won't happen, though. Once again, humans control my destiny.

When they hear of my impending departure, the residents are sad and mope around the house the rest of the afternoon. They throw me a going away party after dinner that brings tears to my big googly eyes. I'm humbled, which is an unfamiliar feeling, by the love and well wishes from all of the guys. All the petting and scratching is a nice touch.

I'm going to miss you guys. I'm sure I'll never look at a homeless person the same way.

The next day, a woman named Maggie loads me into the back seat of her car and drives away.

I don't suppose you'd believe me if I told you my name is Mitch Westcott, and I'm not a dog.

She remains silent, eyes on the road.

I didn't think so.

Our trip ends at a place called the Second Chance Adoption Center. Second chances are great, but I'm already on my third. Or is it my fourth?

She attaches a leash and leads me into a room full of cages.

I think there's been some kind of mistake.

No one listens to me anymore. Luckily, she walks me past the cages through a door and outside to a yard where other dogs are running and playing.

I see a familiar face and run toward him, but I only get a couple of steps before I'm yanked backwards and tumble to the ground.

Maggie laughs. "Hold on a minute." She stoops and releases me from my tether.

I run as fast as my stupid little legs will carry me until I reach him. We stop and stare, then sniff each other.

Clyde! What are you doing here? I thought you'd be dead by now... Wait. That didn't come out right.

It's okay. I know what you mean. Good to see you again, too.

I didn't expect to see anyone I knew here. I can't admit I'm scared. *It's nice to see a familiar face.*

Same here.

I've got a name now. Stella. At first, I hated it, but I guess it's okay.

That's great. I'm still Clyde.

Based on his expression and body language, things hadn't gone so well for him since we parted ways. So, when I tell him about Jim and the shelter, I leave out the good parts, so he won't feel any worse. He didn't say much about how he got here except he'd been adopted by an old man who later passed away.

We hang out together for the rest of our yard time, then move inside to our individual kennels—a word they use here instead of cages—for dinner. My kennel is three doors down from Clyde's, which makes it difficult to continue our conversation.

My neighbor is a long, skinny canine who looks like a hot-dog that sprouted four tiny legs. His face is buried in his dinner. The dog voice in my head scolds me and stops me before I toss out a clever, but derogatory, remark that would have had Mitch's old entourage busting a gut. My time at the homeless shelter taught me not to judge, but old habits die hard.

A bowl of kibble sits in one corner, and I sniff it. I give it one star, two stars below the shelter meals. I miss my shiny, personalized bowl. It remains at the shelter in a place of honor next to a Polaroid Mickey snapped before I left. Those guys are the best.

Oscar Mayer looks up from his bowl, and I bury my face in mine. I don't feel like talking to the neighbors, or anyone for that matter. I'm facing yet another situation I can't control. Mitch controlled his own destiny. The dog voice is back. *Yes, but Mitch was a selfish, entitled—*

Shut up! Dog, or no dog, I'm going to do things my way from now on.

Chapter Sixteen

Clyde is less than enthusiastic about my new take-control attitude.

I'm starting to believe your crazy Mitch story. You don't sound like a dog. You sound like some entitled human who only cares about himself.

At least Mitch was in charge of his own life.

How did that work out?

I have nothing to say. The dog voice in my head has plenty.

Clyde isn't finished. *The sooner you get over yourself and start going with the flow, the better off you'll be.*

I don't trust the flow. I don't like where it's taken me so far.

That's because you've been resisting it. You're paddling upstream, my friend. Perhaps you should try to drop those paddles and enjoy the ride.

I'm angry and frustrated. I shake my head. *I can't enjoy anything anymore.*

Because you're living in the future. Dogs live in the present. They laugh and love and play. Have you ever tried any of those things?

I think I know better than you how I should live my life.

Oh, yeah. I forgot humility.

Look, you do things your way, and I'll do them mine.

Okay, but don't say I didn't warn you.

I turn and walk away. *And I thought he was my friend.*

The rest of the week, I keep to myself. Clyde approaches several times, but I avoid any contact. I don't need any more lectures. In fact, I don't talk to anyone. I spend the time thinking about what my ideal human would look like, and how I can show them I'm not like all the other losers here.

My ugly mug is a handicap I'll have to overcome. I need to work harder and channel my inner Mitch for the charisma and bravado necessary to pull this off. This will be the Stella show, executive producer Mitch Westcott.

The show will open with the star, that's me, positioned to get the best view of potential adopters as they approach. When I see one I like, I rush to center stage using any means possible to push my way to the front, where I put on an irresistible show. I'll have them eating out of my hands. Unless they bring treats, then I'll eat out of theirs.

***

The big day is finally here. It's sunny and the temperature is comfortable, the kind of day that causes humans to visit a nearby park and bring home a new pet. A fence surrounds the large pen I share with a hundred other dogs. The mood is upbeat. The other dogs mill around, unaware of my plan to cherry-pick potential adopters.

I take up my position in the corner of the pen where I can see them walking along the path toward us. The old ones walk while the young ones run ahead. I sense a high level of excitement. This should be... well, a walk in the park. I laugh at my clever remark, confident I will find a new home today.

I evaluate each of the candidates as they approach, eliminating those I feel are unworthy. My criteria include age, demeanor, attractiveness, and how serious they are about owning a pet. Dogs can sense these things. Mitch had similar criteria for women, but not in that order.

A young, attractive couple carrying a toddler catches my eye. I follow them, pushing and shoving my way along the fence.

Stop shoving. I was here first.

You'll get your turn, I say. *This one's mine.*

When they stop, I put on a show they can't resist. But they do, resist that is, and move on. I'm confused and return to my lookout spot. Another wave of people approach, and I identify my next mark. I jump into action, but the result is the same.

As I walk back to my spot, head hanging, someone calls out. "Hey, pug."

I look up to see a hillbilly type who reminds me of Gomer walking toward me. *Apparently, they'll let anybody in here.*

"You're just the dog I've been looking for."

No, I'm not. You must have me confused with some other dog.

He continues to stare. I'm nervous, and I roll my big googly eyes around like I'm half nuts. He frowns. *It's working.* I run around in tight circles, snorting like a locomotive. Out of the corner of my eye, I see him shrug and walk away.

Phew! That was close.

When I'm sure he's gone, I resume my reconnaissance, a little dizzy, but no worse for the wear. That is, until I begin to hallucinate. I think I see Ashley—MY Ashley—walking along the trail. I freeze. She looks older than I remember, and I wonder how much time has passed since Mitch's death.

Dogs don't hold grudges, but she left without saying goodbye. Granted, we'd had a silly fight a few days prior, but couples fight. I blink my gigantic eyeballs, then blink a couple more times. It's her, all right. I finally found her. An explanation would be nice. I need to talk to her, but how?

I remember the last time we spoke and hang my head. It did not go well. She hadn't returned my calls and texts for several days. I didn't know what happened. In retrospect, I probably should have skipped a few drinks before showing up unannounced.

"What are you doing here?"

"We need to talk."

"You're drunk. We'll talk another time, when you're sober."

It's not a no. I should listen to her and come back another time, but this is the first relationship I've had that I might be willing to fight for.

"This can't wait."

"I don't want to talk now. What I want is for you to go home and sleep it off."

"This isn't about what you want."

Her eyes flare. "It never is, Mitch." She steps into the hall and pulls the door until it's only open a crack.

"Is there someone else inside?"

She looks away without a reply.

I feel like a bull, and Ashley just waved a red cape in my face. I raise my voice. "Is there?"

Ashley's dog, Rufus, barks a warning from somewhere inside the apartment.

"If you must know, Nicole and Whitney are here, but that's none of your concern."

I'm pretty sure it is, but I say nothing.

"I don't know if I can do this anymore, Mitch. I need someone who will put me first. I'm tired of competing with you."

"That's a little harsh, don't you think?"

"Sometimes the truth hurts."

I fold my arms across my chest, and my back stiffens. "Are you breaking up with me?"

"I didn't say that. We can talk tomorrow." She places her hands on her hips. "Now, please leave."

"Or what? You'll call the police?"

She shakes her head. "My parents were right about you."

"What does that mean?"

"Goodbye, Mitch."

A few days later, she was gone without a trace. I never spoke to her again.

I blink my big googly eyes and I'm back in the pen watching Ashley and her dog Rufus approach. Rufus could be a problem. He never got along well with Mitch. I used to think it was the dog's fault. Now I'm not so sure.

They're closing in. My heart pounds. *It's showtime!*

Chapter Seventeen

Strutting along the fence, I puff out my chest and push aside anyone who gets in my way. *Move over. Coming through. That's my girl.*

I push a little too hard on my way to the front of the crowd that has gathered center stage and slam into the fence. When I fall backwards, a big dog tries to muscle his way in, and I snap at his leg.

Ashley covers her mouth with her hand while Rufus watches with interest.

"Come on." She tugs at his leash and they move on.

I glare at the big dog. *Now look what you've done!*

Get lost, punk.

I think twice about having another go at him and chase after Ashley instead, but I run out of fence. *Ashley! Come back.* All that comes out is a couple of barks.

She turns, and we make eye contact. It feels like a moment, but all I can do is watch her walk away.

I'm confused again. That didn't go the way I'd planned, but what does a dog have to do? Why is she even here? She already has a dog. Granted, he's big and clumsy and not too smart. Maybe she wants another dog. If she can love a doofus like Rufus, there's still a chance for an ugly dog like me.

As the two disappear into the park, a crushing doubt weighs on me. She doesn't want another dog. She's here for a walk in the park with the one she has. Mitch is just a distant memory, and not a pleasant one, I imagine. Face it. Ashley has moved on.

I hang my head and drag myself to the back of the pen.

Clyde sees me and ambles over. I have no desire to talk to anyone right now.

Please, Clyde. I want to be alone.

You're going about this all wrong... Mitch.

Don't call me that.

Then stop acting like a tool.

He pauses, and our eyes lock. I see no malice.

I'm telling you this as a friend. Humans don't like tools. Especially female humans. They like dogs that are happy and playful and full of love. He leans closer. *And if you really want to make an impression, show some vulnerability. They eat it up. But you have to be sincere. No showboating, just sincerity.*

Clyde is starting to piss me off. *If you're such an expert, why don't I see anyone rushing over here to adopt YOU?*

That's because they're in the tent signing the papers.

What?! You're leaving?

I'm going home... to Lucy and Dan and little Marcus. They're my family now.

Uh... That's great, Clyde. I'm happy for you. I hang my head.

A word of advice?

I exhale. *Okay, lay it on me.*

Start acting like a dog instead of a human.

I think about how well the sad puppy eyes have worked for me in the past, but it's a little late for that. Ashley is gone.

I blew it.

***

My heart isn't in it for the rest of the afternoon. I stay in the back of the pen, wallowing in my misery as I watch a couple of prospects come and go.

A wiseass kid stops and points. "Look at that ugly one in the back."

I know who he's pointing at, and I try to hide. His mother moves him along without a word. If he were my kid, I would have slapped his stupid little face and grounded him for a month. Sadly, it wouldn't change the fact that he was right.

Yikes! Is that what Ashley meant when she said, "Look at that one, Rufus?" Was she too polite to use the word *ugly*, like the little brat did? Kids tend to say what they mean. Adults try to sugarcoat it.

Seeing Ashley again had been a sucker punch. I no longer have the energy to pursue anyone else. As good as it was to see her face and hear her voice, I wish she'd stayed home.

To add insult to injury, I had to watch Clyde leave with his new family. Maybe he was right about my plan. Obviously, it isn't working.

I feel sad and alone when I return to my kennel. Who are they kidding? These are cages. Oscar Mayer's cage is empty and so is the one on the other side of mine. Our numbers have been cut in half. What happens after tomorrow if I'm still here?

I need a plan. Where's that annoying dog voice when you need it? I rest my head on my front legs and remember something Clyde said to me. *If you want to make an impression, show some vulnerability. But you have to be sincere. Start acting like a dog instead of a human.*

I wake up the next morning conflicted, but with a new perspective. I'm a dog now, so I need to act like one. Easier said than done, but I clearly need to try something new. The very thing I've been fighting so hard against might be the only way to survive. Abandoning the remnants of my entitled past and embracing the authenticity of life as a dog is something I need to do, at least until I get adopted.

They transport those of us who are left back to the park for the final day of the event. To counteract my growing anxiety, I study the other dogs and mimic their behavior. I shed my stubborn, isolationist tendencies and join them in playfully milling around inside the pen. Their tails wag and the excitement is contagious, but my stupid little tail doesn't wag like normal dogs. It twitches, so I wiggle my butt to make it more obvious. No one seems to notice my handicap.

I don't play the recon game, content to let fate determine my potential suitors. About an hour into this meet-and-greet, I overhear a young couple inquiring about me to Maggie. I slip into my new charmingly vulnerable identity. It's working until a cute little Lhasa apso steals my spotlight.

I'm discouraged, but not ready to give up. I tell myself it wasn't meant to be. My person is still out there, waiting to bring me home. Clyde had told me that, and he'd been right about everything else. I miss Clyde.

The rest of the morning brings more interest, but no takers. Still, I keep a positive attitude. I've thrown away my paddles, and my boat is moving with the current.

Lunchtime arrives, and they set out bowls of food. A herd of hungry dogs charge the feeding area in the back of the pen. The food's not bad, and I dig in. Before I finish, I hear a familiar voice in the distance.

"Excuse me."

I jerk my face up out of my bowl. *Ashley?*

Maggie, who is standing just inside the fence, walks over to her.

Ashley points at me. "What about that one?"

I'm watching them now. *Which one? This one?*

"Her name is Stella."

That's all I need to hear. Lunch can wait. I run toward my girl.

Ashley watches. "Oh, she must have heard you."

I slow down and stop short of the fence this time. My tail twitches like Elvis on steroids. I sit and look up at her.

"Stella, huh?" She turns to Rufus. "What do you think of this one?"

I don't know. It looks like the crazy one from yesterday.

I probably deserve that for the way Mitch treated him, but I can't let Rufus blow this opportunity for me. *Come on, man, how about giving me a break here? I was having a bad day.*

He stares at me without a word.

"Hi, Stella," Ashley says.

I stand up, tail still twitching, and approach. She puts a couple of fingers through the fence, and I lick them.

"What's her story?" Ashley asks Maggie.

"A friend of mine who works as a social worker at a local homeless shelter brought her in. I'm not sure why, but she lived at the shelter for a while. I guess the residents all loved her, but there were rules about no pets."

"I was here yesterday, and she seemed very aggressive."

That's all in the past. Forget about the past. We can start over. What do you say, Ash?

"I noticed that, but this is the way she's been all week. She's been quiet and has pretty much kept to herself. Jennifer, who brought her here, said she noticed a positive, calming influence on her clients when Stella sat in on her sessions."

"Really? I never would have guessed that yesterday. I'm glad I came back."

Our eyes meet, and for the first time in my life, I feel vulnerable.

"Aww, look at her."

"Do you want to hold her?"

Yes. Please say yes.

"Sure, if that's okay."

Maggie picks me up and hands me to Ashley.

Her fingers ruffle the extra skin on my neck and her hand glides down my back. I'm in heaven. I close my eyes and breathe in her scent. Ashley doesn't need makeup, and rarely wears perfume, but the smell of her shampoo is intoxicating. I pray this moment will never end.

I look down at Rufus, who is clearly not happy. I want to say something but bite my tongue. He looks older than I remember. Perhaps she's here to find his replacement.

Why do we need another dog?

As if she knew what Rufus was thinking, she hugs him. "I have enough love for both of you."

Until she disappears in the middle of the night again and leaves us hanging.

Rufus tilts his head. *What are you talking about?*

She continues. "You won't have to be alone anymore when I go to work. You can train her to be as wonderful a companion as you."

I guess when you put it that way. Rufus licks her face.

I'll take that as a yes. I breathe a sigh of relief. *Attaboy, Rufus.*

Ashley lets go. Rufus turns to me and tilts his head again.

How did you know my name?

CHAPTER EIGHTEEN

Ashley fills out the papers and loads us into her car. Rufus doesn't look convinced when I tell him I overheard Ashley use his name yesterday, but he drops the subject and moves on. I need to find a way to cut him out of the picture.

Sitting in the back seat of Ashley's car, which smells like her shampoo, I'm thinking there really is a God. They say every dog has his day. This must be mine. I wish Clyde could see me now.

We pull up in front of her apartment building. It's nicer than the last one, and I wonder if she has a new job. *Yikes!* And a new boyfriend. Damn it, Mitch. *Maybe if you weren't such a tool!*

Rufus turns. *Are you talking to me?*

Uh... just talking to myself. I'm finding it increasingly difficult to identify with my memories of Mitch.

Getting up the front steps of Ashley's apartment building proves to be a challenge. Not only are my legs inadequate in terms of length, they're about as muscular as pool noodles. Mitch used to play tennis and squash to stay in shape, but that ship has sailed.

Rufus and his long legs climb the stairs with little effort, and he stands at the top, reminding me he's the boss of this outfit. I avoid his glare as he waits with Ashley for me to reach the summit. They watch with amusement.

Inside the building, the hum of the elevator is a welcome sound. No more stairs. The walls have been recently painted and a fresh scent is everywhere. The carpet, while soft and yielding, is teeming with more earthy smells carried in on the shoes of the tenants.

The venue is different, but memories of our hallway skirmish flood back when we reach Ashley's door. The air feels heavy with regret. *What's taking her so long to open the door?* I dance around impatiently, hoping the air inside is lighter.

Rufus stares at me like I'm an escaped mental patient. *Keep your pants on!*

I would if I had any.

It's a little easier to breathe inside. I relax and sniff around her living room. I don't smell a cat, so that's a relief. I get a whiff of strange men coming from the couch, but it's faint, like they've only been here a few times.

"Have a look around, Stella. This is your new home."

She talks to me like I'm a person. I've heard people talk to their pets like they're clueless infants, and it makes me want to stick my paw down my throat. Have a little respect.

I take her up on her offer and head into the kitchen. The lingering food odors are pleasant and the pantry is well stocked. I can work with this. Rufus's bowl sits alone on the floor, and it makes me wish I'd brought mine. I'm sure Ash will get me something soon.

Next stop is the bedroom to check out the sleeping arrangements. Once again, it's a new venue, but a deluge of memories flood my mind. Ecstasy is tempered by sadness and remorse. Then I realize there's someone else inside my head, and it's getting crowded in here. It's like this third entity is Mitch with feelings and, dare I say, some canine qualities. Mitch thought he loved Ashley, but he didn't know what love was. Perhaps the feelings of remorse are because he is learning what love is a little too late.

I shake my head, and Stella is back in control, checking out the room. It's the perfect mix of style and comfort. A stark contrast from the cardboard boxes I've slept in. Pastel colors and warm hues invite you in. An inspirational quote from Marilyn Monroe is framed on one wall. It reads, "Strong women don't have 'attitudes', we have standards." No doubt purchased after she left Mitch.

Rufus has a bed along one wall. Where do I sleep? I picture myself snuggling up against Ashley in the big bed, but I don't want to get ahead of myself.

Ashley is sitting on the couch when I return to the living room. I never thought I'd share a space with Ash. I have to say, it feels good. She still looks hot, but I see her differently now, in ways Mitch couldn't. My dog senses tell me relationships are not about what you can get, but what you can give. It's a foreign concept that may take some time to get used to, but I feel it's worth a shot, given the way things have worked out in the past.

Rufus is bigger than me, but a little on the clumsy side. He lumbers over to cut me off as I toddle across the room toward Ashley.

Where do you think you're going?

His question takes me by surprise. *Uh... nowhere. I thought maybe I'd sit with Ashley on the couch for a bit.*

Well, you thought wrong.

Chapter Nineteen

I study Rufus as he stands in my way. *What have you got against me?*

I don't know yet. Something about you rubs me the wrong way. This is MY house, and I'M in charge. My job is to love and protect Ashley, and that's what I'm going to do.

Protect her? You think she needs protection from me? What about her boyfriend?

I'm watching him like a hawk. Plenty of guys have hurt her after stringing her along.

I hope you're not talking about Mitch, because SHE dumped HIM.

See. That's what I mean. How would you know something like that?

Damage control. I... I... I used to be his dog.

You expect me to believe that?

It's true.

That would be a coincidence of epic proportions. Mitch hated dogs.

Yet, here I am.

He shakes his head. *You can go sit over there by the window.*

As much as I want to lash out at Rufus the doofus, I don't want to cause problems on my first day, so I do as I'm instructed. I recline in such a way that I can keep an eye on both of them.

After a couple of minutes, Ashley pats the cushion next to her. "Come over here, Stella."

I spring to my feet as fast as any pug has ever sprung. I give Rufus the stink eye as I swagger over to the couch like I just won the lottery and bought the building. The smug look slides off my face when I realize the couch is too tall for me to scale.

Fortunately, Ashley doesn't hesitate before she reaches down to give me a boost. I snuggle up close to her hip, and she strokes my back. The smug look returns, and Rufus retreats to the kitchen to drown himself in his water bowl. I'm not sure that's why he went in there, but a dog can dream.

When we're alone, I close my eyes, lean in, and let her fingers work their magic. I don't know whether this is a dog thing, or I'm reliving Mitch's memories of her heavenly hands. Either way, I'm not moving.

"I'm glad you're here, Stella. I think we're going to become best friends."

Are you hearing this, Rufus? Best friends.

"Rufus will teach you everything he knows about being a friend and loyal companion."

Major buzzkill. Everything doofus knows about everything could fit in a shot glass.

"You can keep each other company while I'm at work. He's getting old and will need our help from time to time."

Her fingers lose their magic. *Is that what this is about? You need a playmate and a nursemaid for your dog?*

Rufus is still alive and wanders in from the kitchen. *I guess it's NOT all about you, is it? Oh, yeah... it's all about me.*

The doorbell rings.

"It's Jake." Ashley sets me on the floor and heads for the door.

Jake? From State Farm?

Rufus is quickly by my side. *No, dummy. Jake is the boyfriend.* He shows his teeth in a devious smile. *This should be interesting.*

What do you mean?

Have you ever seen yourself?

I hesitate. Big Dog birthed me, so I have an idea of what I look like, but I've never actually looked in a mirror. *I guess I haven't.*

Follow me. He turns and walks toward the bedroom.

I follow with a mix of curiosity and trepidation.

Inside the room, Rufus pushes the door closed to expose a full-length mirror. *Go ahead, take a look. Just don't break the glass.* He chuckles.

Yikes! That's not a dog, it's a pig.

Rufus laughs. *Your words, not mine.*

What happened to my face? I look like the guy on the bomb squad who cut the wrong wire.

The look on his face tells me he agrees.

This is unacceptable. I need a plastic surgeon.

You're lucky. For some strange reason, Ashley doesn't seem to mind.

It's not all about Ashley. I remember the last time Mitch said that, and I cringe. I stare at the beast in the mirror and hang my head. *Okay, maybe it is.*

Rufus nudges the door open, and we return to the living room to find MY Ashley in another man's arms. I've never seen him before. His enormous eyes, which are almost as big as mine, and his square head, remind me of SpongeBob from that cartoon.

I'm in no mood. I charge them, barking like a rabid dog, but stop just short of biting his leg.

SpongeBob shrieks like a banshee. Ashley covers her mouth with her hand the way she did when I made a fool of myself in the park. This gives me pause, and I back off.

"Stella! Bad dog." She points to a spot on the floor far enough away so SpongeBob can resume breathing. "Sit!"

I hear Rufus laugh from somewhere behind me.

I don't like it, but I do as I'm told. Things were going well, Rufus and the mirror notwithstanding, until Sponge-Bob squeezed his freakishly large head through our door and ruined everything.

Jake points at me. "Is that really a dog?"

Ashley smiles. "Of course it's a dog. Her name is Stella."

"Why is she here?"

"I adopted her to keep Rufus company."

Aww... you shouldn't have. I mean really, you shouldn't have. Rufus gives me a sideways glance. *I was getting along fine on my own.*

"So, you have TWO dogs now?"

Apparently, one dog was too many for Jake. Mitch knew the feeling well. While I empathize with his situation, being a dog offers a different perspective.

Given the look in his eyes, though, one of us needs to go. And let me tell you brother, it ain't gonna be me.

CHAPTER TWENTY

Ashley folds her arms across her chest. "You two need to get along."

I'd rather stick a hot fork in my eye.

Jake's expression tells me he feels the same.

Rufus watches with a look of amusement.

What's so funny?

He just sits there with that dumb look on his face.

How long has she been seeing this Jake guy?

Not long. A couple of weeks, maybe. I don't like him.

Her track record for picking boyfriends is less than stellar.

Rufus scrunches up his face. *I suppose Mitch told you when you were his dog?*

I know everything about Mitch Westcott. By the way, he wasn't your biggest fan.

Let me tell you, the feeling was mutual. Mitch was a tool.

Why does everybody keep saying that? *How do you figure?*

Mitch didn't need a girlfriend, he needed a fan club. Frankly, I don't know how she stayed with him as long as she did.

I growl. *Take that back!*

It's the truth.

That's it. I charge him, which isn't the smartest thing to do, since he's at least twice my size. I bark, and snort, and snap at his leg. He thinks he's smart, but he's older and slower than I am. I slip underneath him where he can't see me and nip at his belly. He's overweight, so it's an easy target.

Rufus lets out a wail, and Ashley runs over to break it up. She pulls us apart, and we watch Rufus, who deserves an Oscar for flailing around the room like the girl in the opening scene of *Jaws.*

Don't be such a baby. I didn't even break the skin.

"Stella! What has gotten into you?"

He started it!

She picks me up and deposits me in the corner. "Now you stay there until I say you can leave."

I feel like a five-year-old kid. I suppose I acted like one. Rufus the doofus knows how to push my buttons. It occurs to me as I sit in the corner, wheezing and pouting, ol' Rufus is dumb like a fox. He doesn't want me here, and he's figured out a way to get rid of me. A couple more provoked attacks like that, and Ashley will be sending me back to the adoption agency.

I won't win an all-out war. I need to find another way. In *The Art of War,* Sun Tzu says, "The greatest victory is that which requires no battle." It means finding non-confrontational solutions and avoiding unnecessary conflicts is a sign of a superior strategy. Clearly, I posses the superior intellect. Where did Rufus go to college? Huh?

I need to get him on my side, or at least convince him that working together can produce a win-win outcome. Unfortunately, I didn't do myself any favors by attacking him.

In the meantime, I have to get back in Ashley's good graces. Given today's incidents with Doofus and SpongeBob, I'm outnumbered and need Ashley on my side. I stare at Ash with big sad eyes, hoping she'll notice me and feel sorry, but I don't like what I see on the couch. Ash and Jake are getting a little too cozy.

I catch a glimpse of Rufus glaring at them and discover a possible solution. Two foes can unite against a common enemy. Jake is that enemy.

My eyes burn after an agonizing half hour of watching Romeo and Juliet fraternize on the couch.

"We're going out for a little while," Ashley says as the two of them stand. "You kids behave while we're gone."

Rufus and I are both on our feet. This can't be good for anybody. I look over at Rufus and catch a frightening it's-payback-time look.

You can't leave me here! I run after them into the hall.

"What are you doing, Stella? Jake and I are going out alone. You need to stay with Rufus."

I can't. Rufus will kill me.

She tries to nudge me back inside with her leg, but I won't budge.

"Do you need some help?" Jake asks.

Stay out of this, SpongeBob.

"Okay, Stella, have it your way," Ashley says. "But I'm on my way to buy you a bed and some new bowls."

Oh. Why didn't you say that in the first place? I stand down. *Why does HE get to go?*

I shuffle back inside and turn around. *Don't listen to anything Jake says. He doesn't like dogs.*

She closes the door, and I'm alone with Rufus, but I don't see him. He's probably planning an ambush. *Rufus? Where are you?*

I check behind the couch. Not there. *Come on, man. You're freaking me out.*

As I head into the kitchen, he charges out of the bedroom. His legs are twice as long as mine, so I don't wait around. I circle the kitchen table a few times, hoping to wear him out, but he keeps coming. I panic when I realize there's no place to hide unless I can make it to the bedroom.

I leave the table's orbit and race across the living room, snorting like a locomotive. We narrowly avoid crashing into the coffee table. I'm worried I won't have enough time to reach the bedroom and close the door behind me.

The sound of glass breaking startles me. I sense the chase is over and stop to take a look.

Rufus sniffs around something on the floor. *Now look what you've done.*

Me?

She loves that vase.

Your big, fat tail knocked it off the coffee table.

Oh yeah? At least I have a tail. That thing on your backside looks like it came from a bag of Cheetos.

Really? Is that the best you've got?

He knocks me to the ground and has me pinned. He glares down at me in a show of dominance.

I get it. You're the alpha dog. You're bigger and stronger than a puppy with stumpy legs and a cheesy tail. Now, can we just get on with our lives?

He lingers for a moment so he can leave on his terms. He eventually backs off, and I crawl out from underneath him. I need some alone time somewhere safe, so I scamper off toward the bedroom. Rufus does not follow.

I close the door behind me and my reflection startles me. *Yikes!* I shake it off and savor the relative peace and quiet. I don't have a proper bed yet, so I pick out a spot on the rug where I can't see the mirror and rest my head. Living with Rufus is exhausting. Something's gotta give.

I'm not getting any closer to finding a way out of this mess. No matter how hard I try, I feel like Dante, in that poem "The Divine Comedy," descending through the nine circles of hell, each one worse than the last. At the beginning of the story, a woman, Beatrice, calls for an angel to bring Virgil to guide Dante on his journey so no harm will befall him.

I drift off to sleep wondering where MY angel is.

When I awake, an angel hovers over me. *At last.* A warmth fills my heart as I feel her heavenly hands stroke my stomach. My eyes focus, and I realize my angel is Ashley. She's back, and for the moment I feel safe from Rufus's wrath.

"Rufus tells me you broke my vase."

Me? He's the one who...

I look at Rufus. He's smiling like the Cheshire Dog, if that's even a thing. I know there was a cat. *You told her? How is that even possible?*

When you know someone as long as I've known Ashley, you don't need words.

Despite the presence of an angel, I feel myself descending to the next circle.

Chapter Twenty-One

Ashley surprises me with her handling of the broken vase.

"I didn't care for that old thing anyway."

Interesting. Rufus either lied about her feelings for the vase or he doesn't know her as well as he thinks he does.

"You need to be more careful around my things from now on. No running or jumping in the house."

Jumping? Is that what you think I did? Have you seen my legs? I can't jump rope, let alone onto a coffee table. She's barking up the wrong tree, so to speak. *I'm not the bad guy here. I was running for my life. Perhaps you should have a little talk with John Wick over there.*

Rufus sends a this-isn't-over glare my way.

As much as I hate to apologize for something I didn't do, I don't want to risk her turning me away... again. Rufus is proving to be a challenge, but I realize I've been given another chance with Ash, albeit a platonic one. I love her and want to make this work.

I lower my head and look up at her with sorrowful eyes.

"Aww." Ashley sits on the floor and motions for me to join her.

I shuffle over and she sets me in her lap, where her magic fingers make everything better.

Rufus leaves the room.

"I know you'll do better. It's only our first day together."

For the next few minutes, we sit in blissful silence, my tail moving against her thigh. *I'll do better, Ash. I promise.*

It's the first time I'm thankful for this canine disguise. I have a feeling it's becoming more than a disguise.

"Let's go into the other room so I can show you what I bought."

She sets me down, and I follow. Two shiny new bowls sit on the hardwood floor next to what appears to be a dog bed, barely visible beneath Rufus.

"Rufus! Get out of there. That's for Stella."

Mine's bigger, he says.

So is your ass.

I sniff the bowls and then the bed.

"Well, what do you think?"

I think they're great. The bed might need to air out a bit before I can sleep on it.

"Try it out."

I don't want to disappoint her, so I hold my breath, climb aboard, and lie down. A couple of quick barks let her know I approve.

She also bought me my first collar and leash—which I could do without.

I need to go outside soon, or she'll have a mess to clean up, so I walk to the door, look at her and bark.

She smiles. "You need to go out now? Good girl. Come on, Rufus, we're all going for a walk."

Why does he have to come?

You're not a stray anymore. Someone needs to show you how to behave in the real world.

And you think you're that dog?

Like it or not, I'm all you've got.

When everyone is tethered, Ashley opens the door, and Rufus leads our posse down the hall and into the great outdoors. The air smells fresher, and I walk a little taller beside Ashley. I belong to someone now. That's right, I'm talking about the babe on the other end of my leash.

Rufus is busy sniffing everything in sight. I've learned that's what dogs do, so I follow suit.

I need to relieve myself, so I stop at the next tree and squat.

Hold it right there. Rufus runs over. *That's my tree.*

Really? I don't see your name carved into it anywhere.

It's called etiquette, something you'll need to learn if you want to survive out here.

I figured it's first come, first served.

Give it a good sniff.

I give the base of the tree a few sniffs. *Yuck! Smells like a big doofus. I guess it IS your tree after all.*

Now, get out of my way.

Rufus lifts his leg and wets the side of the tree. *It's called marking your territory. This is my tree. Any dog with an ounce of integrity will move along and find his own tree.*

What if the trees are all taken?

There's plenty of trees. You need to find one to make your own.

I don't want to seem helpless, but I really need to go. *Do you know of any unmarked trees in the area?*

You're a female. You don't need a tree.

Excuse me?

You can squat anywhere.

Anywhere?

Anywhere in the grass out here.

Why didn't you tell me that earlier?

You didn't ask.

I shuffle a few feet away from the tree into the grass, as far as the leash will allow. *How's this?*

Too close.

I look at Ash, standing at the other end of the taut leash. *Just pull on it, she'll follow you.*

It works. I pull, she follows. *How's this?*

Make sure it's not taken.

I sniff around. Nothing but grass.

"Is that it?" Ashley asks when I'm through.

Unfortunately, no.

Mitch was no stranger to public urination, mostly after he'd had a few drinks. It's the other that has taken some getting used to. I'm embarrassed, but I have no choice.

Come on, Ash, look the other way. Please?

You'd better get used to it, princess. We can't go back inside until you do your business. She's seen me go a hundred times. Besides, you'll get a treat if you go.

When I finish with my business, Ashley picks it up in a plastic bag, which makes it ten times more humiliating. Being a *good dog* doesn't always feel so good. Rufus is amused by my embarrassment.

Ashley offers me a chewy dog treat that taste like meat. It doesn't do much for my self-esteem.

I look at Rufus. *You call that a treat?*

What were you expecting?

Some chocolate would be nice. It's my favorite.

Are you nuts? Dogs can't eat chocolate.

Seriously? This just keeps getting better and better.

It's poison. You could die.

Uh... I meant it smells good. If I were a human, it would be my favorite.

Despite my fears to the contrary, Ashley seems pleased and not the least bit embarrassed by my public humiliation. I guess it's something I need to learn to accept. That, and not eating chocolate.

All in all, it's been a decent outing. The fact that Rufus had been willing to help me navigate our little business trip made me think he might be coming around... until we get back to the apartment.

CHAPTER TWENTY-TWO

I thought perhaps Rufus and I had turned a corner in our relationship, but when we arrive home, Dr. Jekyll turns into Mr. Hyde. We're eating dinner in the kitchen when Rufus knocks me over and spills my bowl. He returns to his food before Ashley rushes in from the living room.

"Stella! Look at the mess you've made."

I devour the spilled food as fast as I can for fear she will banish me to a far corner of the apartment where I'll starve for the rest of the evening. I push the bowl out of the way, and it hits the refrigerator, clanging and spilling more.

"Stella! Stop it."

Apparently, this is not the appropriate response.

"Bad dog."

I hate when she calls me that.

Rufus had gotten me good this time. He's on a mission to have me sent away. Besides the fact that Rufus is much bigger than me, any future signs of aggression toward him will not help my case. Somehow, Operation Goodbye Stella must be stopped before his plan gains any more momentum. But how?

When I look up, Jake appears at Ashley's side.

When did he get here?

"What did I tell you, Ash? She's nothing but trouble. You don't need another dog."

"Who asked you?"

Jake frowns. "What?"

"Go sit in the other room while I clean this up."

Trouble in paradise?

I glance at Rufus, who is minding his own business... like a good dog.

Hey, Doofus! This has got to stop.

If you don't like it, you can leave.

I watch Ashley clean up the last bits of kibble from the floor and pick up my bowl. *It's not that simple.*

Sure it is.

In a bold move, I decide to tell him why. This is either going to make things a little better, or a lot worse.

I wasn't Mitch's dog. Skipping any more preamble, I blurt it out. *I was, I mean I am, Mitch.*

I knew there was something wrong with you. You're batshit crazy.

It's the truth. As far as I can tell, Mitch died and was somehow reborn as a dog.

Rufus tilts his head. *What? That's impossible.*

That's what I thought, but here I am. That day in the park... Ashley never mentioned your name. I knew it because I'd been to her apartment when we were dating.

What's going on here? He takes a step back.

I can prove it. Ask me anything about Mitch.

Uh...

Okay, I'll go first. Remember that little rubber penguin? You used to chew on it all the time. Squeak, squeak, squeak. It drove me crazy! Then suddenly, it disappeared, didn't it? Mitch took it. No more squeaking.

What do you know about the time I got lost? he asks.

Which one? The concert in the park, the beach, or the downtown festival? If I recall, somehow your leash came untied, and you wandered off. Mitch, Mitch, and Mitch.

What's Mitch's favorite food?

Pizza.

What about mine?

Bacon.

Rufus hesitates. *Wait a minute. I know what this is. I'm being punked, right? Oh, that's a good one... you're Mitch. Where's the camera?*

There is no camera. I'm telling you the truth.

He stares at me for a minute. *I could make your life miserable like Mitch made mine...*

I'm second-guessing this strategy.

Maybe I will... if I ever stop laughing.

His legs give out and he falls to the floor. He rolls around, squealing and snorting and breathing so heavily I think he might hyperventilate. When he comes up for air, he studies me before speaking.

So, the mighty Mitch Westcott is a female dog? And an ugly one at that.

This is immediately followed by another round of rolling, squealing, snorting, and heavy breathing.

I bark. *Come on, man. We've got a problem here.*

Ashley appears in the doorway. "Rufus. What's the matter?"

He stops.

I squeeze my enormous eyes shut and open them, hoping this is a bad dream.

We? I think you're the one with the problem, Rufus says before he looks up at Ash.

She leans over and pats his head, then looks into his big dopey eyes. "Are you feeling okay? You're a good dog. I'll get you some more water."

You think HE'S the good dog? Come on, Ash, don't let him fool you.

She places the bowl on the floor and watches Rufus lap it up, splashing half of it on the floor.

Yeah, there's your good dog, all right.

He finishes his water, and we're alone again. *So, what's the big problem?*

The way I see it, we have two. The first is you and your hostile attitude toward me, because we need to work together on the second, even bigger problem.

Really? What's that?

Jake. He's gotta go.

Ashley is too good for this guy, just like she was too good for Mitch. As much as it still hurts to say this, I don't believe Ashley should be without a man in her life. I just think I need to be involved in the hiring process.

Rufus tilts his head. *Is that Mitch talking, or Stella?*

Forget about Mitch. We need to work together to help Ashley. I thought you said that was your job.

A door slams, and the sound echoes through the apartment.

Rufus peeks into the living room. *He's gone.*

I join him. *Good riddance.*

He'll come back. They always do.

I watch Ash take a seat on the couch. *We can't let that happen.*

She thinks if she doesn't find someone soon, she never will, so she's willing to settle.

That's crazy.

Ashley stares off into space, looking like she's about to burst into tears. I have to do something. I run toward her as fast as my little legs will take me. In an unprecedented move, I attempt to leap onto the cushion beside her.

I crash headfirst into the front of an unforgiving couch, flattening my face even more than nature had intended. I yelp.

"Oh, Stella! Are you hurt?"

Only my pride.

She scoops me up and sets me next to her. "Just ask if you want to come up here. I'll help you." Her magic fingers chase away my pain and embarrassment.

Rufus joins us, and we bookend her on the couch as she silently stares at an undetermined spot on the opposite wall. Eventually, she speaks.

"What's wrong with me?"

Nothing. Nothing's wrong with you. You're too good for that loser. Who doesn't like dogs, right?

Mitch.

Not now, Rufus.

"What would I do without you two?"

CHAPTER TWENTY-THREE

Ashley wasn't herself for the rest of that day and the next. She leaves for work on Friday without her phone.

Rufus seems out of sorts, as well. He's been sleeping more than usual and acting a little mopey. I can't tell if it's because of Ash, or he has something else going on. I should just enjoy the peace and quiet, but I feel lonely and helpless. Ash needs something I can no longer give her. Unfortunately, Mitch was unable, or unwilling, to provide that something when he had the chance. So, here we are.

Ashley's phone rings on the end table where she'd left it. Another attempt to leap onto the couch at this point would be ill-advised.

Rufus. Jump up there and see who's calling.

Me? But I can't read.

And I can't jump. Stop your whining and knock it off onto the floor so I can see it.

Rufus shuffles over to the table, rears up on his hind legs and paws at the phone until it slides off onto the floor.

One missed call from Jake. *Oh, no, you don't.* I swipe the screen with my nose and the notification disappears.

What's going on?

Jake called.

What are we going to do?

The phone rings again, and I tap my nose on the red *dismiss* button.

That!

It rings a few minutes later, and again I clear it. *I can do this all day, Jake.*

What if he calls tomorrow when she has her phone?

Hopefully, after a few more times, he'll get the message that she never wants to speak to him again. Mitch didn't, and look where it got him.

When the phone rings again a half hour later, my big flat face accidentally taps the *answer* button.

"Hello? Ashley? Why aren't you answering my calls?"

I take a step back. *Yikes!*

We stare at it as Jake's voice gets louder and more insistent.

I can't take it anymore. I shout, *You're done, loser. She never wants to see you again, so stop calling!* What he hears is, WOOF, WOOF, WOOF! I'm sure it lost something in the translation, but the intent would have been hard to miss.

The diatribe spewing from the phone stops.

Yeah, that's right, I'm talking to you. I turn to Rufus. *Say something.*

After a bit of hesitation, he says, *Dogs rule!*

The screen goes black.

Dogs rule?

You put me on the spot.

We stare at each other for a moment, then laugh. Admittedly, it doesn't sound like much, but we're laughing hard inside. Apparently, he's feeling a little better.

The laughter ends when the phone rings again. I dismiss the call.

As far as anybody here is concerned, that never happened.

Rufus tilts his head. *What never happened?*

Exactly.

You really do want to protect her, don't you?

Of course. I love her. Always will.

I'm learning the real meaning of that word. It feels good, so I figure I'm on the right track.

Rufus hangs his head and shuffles off to his bed.

I call after him. *That's a good thing, right?*

Yes.

Then, what's the matter?

I'm just tired. I'm going to lie down.

The phone rings again. I dismiss the call and rest my head on my paws, waiting for the next one.

After a few more thwarted attempts, I have trouble keeping my eyes open.

"Stella..."

What?! Where am I?

"Mommy is home."

If you ever say that again, I'm going to poop on your pillow.

"What are you doing sleeping on the floor?"

A rhetorical question, I assume.

"There's my phone!" She sits cross-legged on the floor next to me like she wants to play. *Who are you, and what have you done with the zombie who left here this morning without her phone?*

"What a good dog. You've been guarding it for me. You can't imagine how naked I felt without it all day."

I zoned out after "good dog"... until she got to "naked."

"Good. I didn't miss any calls."

None that were important, anyway.

"Where's Rufus?"

Does she honestly think I'll answer one of these times? Bless her heart. I nuzzle her leg, and my tail vibrates like an old refrigerator. *Forget about him. Let's cuddle.*

"Rufus, where are you? Come here, boy."

Rufus drags himself out of the bedroom and stands in front of her with his head hung low.

"You don't look so good. Are you all right?"

He's been like that all day. Probably just backed up. We should go for a walk.

"Maybe you need some fresh air."

Great minds think alike. Look alive, Rufus. We're going for a walk. My tail shifts into the next higher gear.

She's in a good mood. I wonder what happened.

In the hall, I watch Ashley and wonder if there are any eligible bachelors living here in the building. I find it amusing to think Mitch would be trying to fix his girlfriend up with another guy. I'm distracted by the scent of something delicious as we pass apartment 2B and linger for a moment.

Ashley tugs on my leash. "Come on, Stella."

I vote we find out who lives here and invite ourselves for dinner tonight.

Another tug and we're moving again.

Outside, we wander the streets for some time before Rufus and I each find appropriate spots to take care of our respective business. Rufus seems more alert and a little lighter on his feet afterward.

"Come on, guys. We need to get back and get dinner started. I'm having company tonight."

I pick up the pace, eager to get home for dinner. *Wait. What company?* It better not be a new boyfriend. I haven't had time to begin my recruiting efforts.

I look over at Rufus, but he's minding his own business with his nose to the ground.

The scent I'd detected on the way out of the building hangs deliciously in the second-floor hall when we return. I pause to take it in, which earns me a look from Ashley and another tug. When she turns back around, she bumps into a man coming out of 2B.

They each take an awkward step backward.

"I'm sorry. I didn't see you coming," he says.

"Not your fault. I should watch where I'm going."

My protective instinct takes over, and I step between them, but I'm distracted by the smell of his clothes. *Delicious.* I'm moving and sniffing and tangling his legs in my leash.

The man smiles. "Is this your dog?"

Ashley stifles a laugh. "It's that obvious, huh?" She takes a knee and unhooks my tether. "I think she likes you."

I slip through his open door to have a look around inside his apartment, hoping to find a woman at the stove passing out samples of the five-star meal she's cooking up. But the place is empty.

"Stella! Come out here."

"It's okay. Probably just hungry."

Back in the hall, I size this guy up. I'm not in the habit of rating men, but he's a solid eight.

"I'm Tyler," he offers.

"Ashley." She points down the hall. "I'm in 2D."

"Nice to finally meet you, Ashley in 2D."

"Finally?"

"I've seen you around the building. I recognize the big dog, but this one must be new."

"About a week. My friends can't understand why I would want a pug. I think they're cute in a quirky and oddly charming sort of way."

"More like George Jefferson than George Clooney, I'd say."

"Exactly." She smiles. I remember that smile. "Except this one's a she. Stella."

Tyler stoops to scratch behind my ears, which is another way to this dog's heart. "Oddly charming... I have to agree with you. Perhaps you need new friends."

You're both half nuts.

He stands, and an awkward moment hangs in the air.

Rufus, you seeing this?

Yeah. So what?

"Well," Ashley says. "We'd better get going."

What? Ask him if we can stay for dinner.

"I guess I'll see you around."

"I guess you will."

So, THAT just happened. This Tyler guy has potential.

Inside the apartment, Ash closes the door and leans back against it. A small, secret smile flashes across her lips.

It appears Ashley shares my enthusiasm.

Chapter Twenty-Four

Ashley must have felt guilty after smelling whatever Tyler had on the stove. She makes us ground beef and rice, which falls a little short in comparison, but tastes a step or two above the usual kibble.

After dinner, she straightens up the apartment before her company arrives. Rufus tells me two friends she knew from Westport come around from time to time to drink wine and spill their guts about everything from shoes to their love lives, but mostly the latter. I find myself interested in every detail of Ashley's life now and look forward to a front-row seat for tonight's event. It isn't eavesdropping if you do it in plain sight.

The girls arrive around seven. They look vaguely familiar. Two bottles of wine and three glasses are on the coffee table, along with some finger food. It smells good, so I wander by, but get shooed away.

"Those aren't for you."

Probably because I don't have fingers. My presence earns me an introduction. I can tell by the looks on their faces they're not impressed. The girls' names are Nicole and Whitney. These were the two at Ashley's apartment the night I showed up drunk.

I've had much more practice rating women than men. Whitney is an easy eight. Nicole, who is a little rough around the edges, isn't far behind at seven and a half. All in all, the girls make a good-looking trio.

The chatter begins once the wine is poured. Mostly who's hot and who's not, who's doing who, and other sordid details. As the wine flows more freely, so does the conversation.

While Rufus snores in the corner, my eyes are wide open, which isn't unusual given my anatomy. They take turns dishing about their respective love lives. Some of the things coming out of Nicole's mouth would make a sailor blush. I didn't know women talked like that.

I hear Mitch's name and try to look uninterested.

"He was gorgeous," Whitney says. "He just wasn't a catch."

"More like catch and release."

The two laugh. Ashley sips her wine.

I want to make them stop.

"Men like Mitch are good for a week or two of good times—not the kind you want to settle down with."

"He was a tool, Ash. He'd been breaking hearts all over town."

That's the Mitch I remember.

Shut up, Rufus.

"You didn't know him like I did. He wasn't as bad as all that."

Then why did you up and leave the way you did?

"I'm proud of you girl," Nicole says. "You dropped him like a hot potato, even if you waited longer than I would have."

"Nicole!" Whitney places her hand on Ashley's arm. "Don't listen to her."

Ashley empties her glass and sets it down. "He's dead. Can we talk about something else?"

"Mitch would have enjoyed his funeral," Nicole continues. "He loved being the center of attention."

"I would have gone, but I couldn't face his family."

You didn't go to my funeral?

"I felt responsible for his death."

What?!

"It wasn't your fault," Whitney says.

"He had it coming."

That's a little harsh, Nicole. Say something, Ash.

Instead of responding, she pours herself another glass.

I've seen enough. Time to change the subject. At the risk of sounding like Mitch, it's time to talk about ME. I run toward the couch and attempt to jump into Ashley's lap. I don't expect to make it, but I have to stop all the Mitch bashing.

He probably deserves some of it, but these so-called friends are making my girl uncomfortable.

Another epic fail lands me on the floor at Ashley's feet. The room is silent for a moment.

"What's wrong with your dog?"

"That had to hurt," Whitney says when they stop laughing.

I right myself and shake away the little stars that are swimming around in my eyes. *It's called taking one for the team.*

Nicole stares at me. "Where did you get this crazy dog?"

"She's not crazy. She's... physically challenged. She was trying to jump up here." Ashley picks me up and deposits me in her lap. "I think it's sweet."

"I think it's crazy."

Well, at least I managed to change the subject... and get a little love for my trouble. My neck is going to be stiff for a couple of days, but this lap therapy is good for both of us.

It doesn't take them long to get back to grilling Ashley about her current romantic situation.

"You haven't mentioned Jake. Are you two still a thing?"

"I don't think so."

Nicole makes a dismissing motion with her hand. "Good riddance."

That's what I said.

Whitney frowns. "What happened?"

"We had a fight. He's been calling, but I just can't bring myself to jump back in."

Did you hear that, Rufus? We did it.

"Good for you." Nicole raises her glass. "Next week, we're all going on a manhunt."

"I don't know." Ashley shakes her head. "I think I just need some time for me."

"Maybe we should let her recover for a minute," Whitney says, looking at Nicole.

"No. She doesn't need to recover. I know that look. She found someone."

"Ash?" Whitney waits for confirmation.

Maybe she just wants to spend some quality time with her new dog.

Yeah, I'm sure that's it.

Shut up, Rufus.

"No, I haven't found anyone. I'm not even looking."

"That's when the magic happens," Whitney says.

Nicole refills her glass. "I'm never not looking."

My eyes get heavy, so I find a comfortable spot on Ashley's lap to rest my head. My ears are up in case someone mentions Mitch again.

I must have dozed off, because when I open my eyes, Ashley and I are alone on the couch. Two empty wine bottles sit on the coffee table in a quiet room. She's staring at something on the opposite wall. Mitch never knew the right thing to say in situations like this. A dog can say the right thing without saying anything at all.

We sit there for a while, the warmth of our bodies comforting each other. I can do this all night if that's what she needs.

Eventually, she breaks out of her trance and picks me up. She holds me up in front of her face until we're only inches apart. Instinct takes over, and I lick her face. It feels good and tastes even better. She flinches a little but doesn't pull away. I do it again. She lets out a playful laugh, then pulls back to study me.

"You ARE a funny-looking creature, aren't you?"

I'm aware. But I'm okay with it if you are. I stare into her beautiful eyes and drink in the smell of her shampoo.

"One of my old boyfriends used to look at me like that."

You better be talking about Mitch.

"Poor, Mitch. He was a hot mess, but I believed he had potential."

Then why did you leave?

"I saw something decent inside him, but he was too stubborn and self-centered to let it out. Now, he'll never get the chance."

Never say never.

A tear rolls down her cheek.

Don't cry. Mitch will get over it, and so will you. Mistakes are a part of life. Take it from a funny-looking dog, you learn to accept what is and move forward from there. You're a catch, Ash. The right man will come along.

"What should I do, Stella?"

You made a few mistakes. Tomorrow is a new day.

"I wish you could talk to me."

You and me both.

She sighs. "It's exhausting."

She rests her head on a cushion and pulls me in close. "I'm too tired to get ready for bed. Will you stay here with me tonight?"

She doesn't have to ask twice.

CHAPTER TWENTY-FIVE

This is the best night of the entire six months I've been a dog. Not only do I get to spend the entire night lying next to my Ashley, I don't have to share a room with Rufus, who farts like a rhino. The one that got away is back in my life. I won't make the same mistake twice.

The warmth of her body and the rhythmic rise and fall of her breathing lulls me into a trance-like state. Pleasant thoughts of our future together float through my mind like puffy white clouds on a summer day. Then they're gone, replaced by the echoes of Ashley's two so-called friends bashing Mitch. I'd waited for Ash to come to his rescue, but she remained silent. Apparently, everything they'd said was true. My previously myopic attitude blinded me from the truth until now. I'm forced to face the harsh reality that Mitch really was a tool.

It's time for me to grow a pair, figuratively speaking of course, and let the vestige of my former self go. I am Stella now, a dog—a good dog—who belongs to Ashley, whom I will love, honor, and obey until death do us part. It feels good to finally say something like that. I snuggle a little closer and drift off to sleep.

The morning light brings an intruder into our midst.

What's going on here?

I open my eyes to see Rufus sniffing around. *What does it look like? We had a sleepover.*

He climbs up on the couch and wakes Ashley.

Now look what you've done, I say, disturbed by his meddling. *Leave us alone.*

Ashley yawns and rubs her eyes. "What's going on?"

That's what I'd like to know, Rufus says.

I don't move, clinging to my last few moments next to her.

"I must have had too much wine last night," she says, her hand on her forehead. "Thank you for staying here with me, Stella."

Give me a break, Rufus says.

"Rufus. Get down off the couch."

My tail twitches like Elvis singing "Hound Dog."

He jumps, but his legs crumple beneath him, and he goes down in a heap.

Ashley rushes to his side, leaving me alone on the couch. "Are you okay, Rufus?"

Faker!

She strokes his back and examines his legs.

He catches my glare, and I expect to see a shit-eating grin on his face, but I see only fear. I'm stuck on the couch, afraid to jump to the floor and risk duplicating Rufus's face-plant. I bark, and Ashley deposits me on the floor. It isn't until I cautiously sniff around his head, that I realize he's in distress.

Sorry. I thought it was a stunt to get some attention.

I don't know what happened. My legs just stopped working. I'm scared.

I'd never seen him like this. My canine instincts take over, and I nuzzle the back of his neck for moral support. *I'm sure you'll be okay. Can you stand up now?*

He pulls himself up on two legs, and Ashley helps him the rest of the way.

Atta boy!

He takes a couple of tentative steps without incident.

"That's better. Let's get you some water."

I follow them into the kitchen, where Ash fills his water bowl. Rufus drains it.

"You were probably just dehydrated. Maybe you should take it easy for a while. Stella will keep an eye on you while I'm at work."

That won't be necessary.

Ashley's right. I'll find you a nice spot under the window. The sunlight will make you feel better.

We mosey over to the perfect spot, and he curls up on the carpet. I'd never moseyed before, but it seemed appropriate here, given Rufus's condition. I sit nearby and keep a watch-ful eye.

Stop staring. You're making me nervous.

Ashley said to keep an eye on you.

You plan to sit there like that all day?

If I have to.

He studies me. *You don't sound like Mitch.*

That's because I'm not Mitch. I'm Stella.

Rufus continues to stare without a word.

This is not a good sign, Rufus says. *I don't think I have too long to live.*

Come on, man. Don't talk like that. This is temporary—like turbulence on a cross-country flight. Just stay in your seat and ride it out.

Everything hurts.

You did a face-plant off the couch. I'd be surprised if every-thing DIDN'T hurt.

You're still young. You'll see. Dogs can sense these kinds of things.

I'm not sure what to say.

Rufus lays his head down and lets out a sigh.

I continue my vigil. What if he's right about his ability to sense death? Mitch's death happened so fast, he never saw it coming. It must be awful to know death is imminent. Even if he's mistaken, he'll spend the rest of his life looking over his shoulder for the grim reaper.

After a while, he falls asleep. I keep an eye on him like a good dog until he farts. It smells like death, and I have to get up and walk it off. Shortly after I return to my post, I drift off to sleep.

I'm not good with time, so I don't know how long I've been asleep. Rufus hasn't moved. I berate myself for falling asleep. Anything could have happened while I napped.

Ashley left food out for us. Time to eat. We both need to keep up our strength. I get up and shuffle over to check on him. He doesn't move as I approach. Is he breathing? Oh no. What have I done? I sniff around him but find nothing sinister.

Rufus! Wake up. I nudge him. Still no movement. *Come on, man. You can't die on my watch.*

I take a few steps back and run headfirst into his stomach.

Hey! What'd you do that for?

I thought you were dead.

Try that again, and you'll be the dead one.

Come on. We need to go eat something.

I'm not hungry.

Ashley left us food because you didn't eat much last night.

Rufus doesn't respond.

I'll give you a treat if you eat something. Did I really just say that?

What kind of treat?

Those little cookies shaped like bones. I know where Ashley keeps them.

Rufus stares at me for a moment like he's considering my offer. *Okay.*

In the kitchen, I sniff around a lower cupboard where I'd seen Ashley stash the dog treats. The door doesn't line up properly, leaving a small gap I hope to exploit. I paw at it, but the latch won't give up its hold.

Step aside, Rufus says.

What have I got to lose? I oblige.

He charges the door and rams it with his shoulder. The latch lets go and the door springs open. The impact jars the items inside, and the box of dog treats falls and spills its contents on the floor.

Rufus must be feeling better, because he sucks them up like a new Hoover.

Hey! You were supposed to eat something.

I did. A bunch of little bone-shaped cookies.

Outsmarted by a doofus, I cut my losses and push a couple out of his reach, saving them for myself.

The rest of the afternoon is uneventful under my watchful eye. I run to Ashley as soon as she walks through the door. *Boy, am I glad you're home. I don't think I can be trusted to watch Rufus all day.*

"Hi, Stella. Who's a good dog? Are you happy to see me?"

I forget she can't understand me. All she hears is "woof, woof, woof!"

I'm always happy to see you. But something's wrong with Rufus. I can smell it. I thought he died this afternoon. He could go any minute. You gotta help him.

"Where's Rufus? Did you keep an eye on him like I asked?"

I tried, Ash. I really did, but I'm just a little dog. Frankly, it's a big ask.

Rufus shuffles over.

"There you are." She hugs him. "You're a good dog, too. Do you feel better?"

Rufus licks her face.

"I'll take that as a yes."

I'm helpless to add my take on the situation.

"Give me a minute, and then we'll all go for a walk."

I know I need a walk, but I'm worried about Rufus's condition.

Maybe a walk is too much for you right now.

I've got some important business to take care of, as I'm sure you do, too.

Yes, but I'm worried about you.

I'm perfectly fine. Didn't you hear Ashley? I'm a good dog.

Good dogs don't lie.

CHAPTER TWENTY-SIX

Our walk is uneventful, and we take care of business in the usual manner. I watch Rufus like a hawk. He never says a word. Back in the apartment, he seems a little more like himself, but I know something is off.

Ashley leaves me in charge again the following day and the weight of the responsibility is crushing. I want to tell her she needs to make other arrangements, but my tongue is tied, so to speak. She's a nurse, someone accustomed to caring for sick people, but I'm just a funny-looking little dog who can't even take care of myself. Rufus is twice my size and unwilling to listen to anything I say. What could possibly go wrong?

I hold my own for the next two days. Rufus is getting back to his old self, but not enough to chase me around and break anything. Operation Goodbye Stella appears to have been called off, or at least put on hold. Perhaps he's realized I'm not going anywhere and we need to get along for Ashley's sake.

When Ashley gets home, I get a little extra lovin' because the place is in order and Rufus is still alive. Who's a good dog now?

Instead of rattling pots and pans in the kitchen, Ashley refills our bowls and disappears into her bedroom. I still feel an obligation to monitor Rufus's activities. I finish my dinner and check on him.

Come on, Rufus, you need to eat.

I said, I'm not hungry.

I have no more tricks up my sleeve after Ashley found the half-empty box of dog treats on the floor the other day and fixed the broken latch on the cupboard. However, I do have a superior intellect—a holdover from my previous life.

Suit yourself, but if you're not going to eat it, I will.

I wouldn't do that if I were you.

We can't just let it go to waste, especially when I'm still hungry. I stick my face in his bowl and come up with a mouthful.

He charges at me, pushes me out of the way, and empties the bowl. He gets up in my face when he finishes. *Too bad you're still hungry, huh?*

Yeah, too bad.

Rufus is clueless.

I wander into the bedroom to check on Ashley. The bathroom door is closed, and I hear the shower. That's not unusual. She will sometimes shower after work when she's had a bad day.

I consider lying down in my bed and waiting for her to come out, but quickly dismiss the idea. I'm proud of myself for not taking advantage of my situation and hanging around in her room whenever she changes her clothes. Female dogs don't care about such things, but my inner Mitch, well, that's a different story.

I retreat to the living room to look for Rufus. *What's up with Ash?*

Maybe she had a bad day at work.

Yeah, that's it. She'll probably come out any minute to make herself some dinner and hang out with us.

I smell her perfume drifting out into the living room and realize she won't be eating at home tonight. An invisible fist punches me in the gut. *She's going out to dinner. With a dude.*

That's usually what that smell means.

My heart rate is up, and my paws are sweating. *Do you know who it is?*

Jake?

I thought he was history.

Maybe someone new.

She needs to run that by us first.

Unfortunately, that will never happen. It's frustrating. I'm not saying I know what's best for her, but you have to admit, she doesn't have the best track record with men.

She looks like a million bucks when she finally emerges from her bedroom.

Wow! Looking good, Ash. I hope you're not wasting it on another loser.

The doorbell rings as she's slipping on a pair of fancy shoes. "That must be Walter."

Wait a minute. Walter? This can't be good for anybody.

She ushers him in and introduces him to Rufus and me.

I give him the once-over. *I'm afraid not, Ash. You can do better.*

While Tyler's a solid eight, this guy is a weak seven. The fact that he isn't wearing a bow tie helps his score. He presents Ashley with a bunch of flowers he'd been hiding behind his back, like he'd just stepped out of the 1950s, which is around the time his name was popular.

I remind myself that looks aren't everything—a lesson I learned the hard way.

Ashley puts the flowers in water and says her goodbyes before the unlikely couple disappears into the night. I'd give anything to tag along so I can chaperone.

As their footsteps fade in the hall, I park myself in front of the door and begin my vigil. I've learned dogs can sit for hours with little or no effort. I've also learned they sleep a lot. Eventually, my big googly eyes refuse to stay open. Some time later, I'm awakened by a nudge, then another.

"Stella, is that you? Let me in."

I jump to my feet, which isn't very far, and step aside.

"Aww, you've been waiting for me. Did you miss me?"

She slips off her shoes and bends down. Her bracelets rattle like wind chimes as she strokes my back.

I can see down her neckline. *Of course I missed you, but right now, I'm not missing anything. I hope you weren't giving Walter any freebies. That's not a first date dress, by the way.*

Somewhere in the back of my mind, Mitch disagrees.

"I missed you, too." She stands. "Where's Rufus? He usually greets me at the door."

He went to bed hours ago. I think something's wrong with him. He doesn't smell right.

Ashley needs to unwind, so I sit with her on the couch and watch TV for a while before we go to bed.

Rufus smells better in the morning, and I wonder if I overreacted.

What happened last night? Rufus asks.

I don't know what time she got home, but I think it was late.

You fell asleep, didn't you?

Asks Rip Van Winkle. Ashley said you usually greet her at the door. What happened?

None of your business.

I think you're too stubborn to admit you're getting old.

This isn't about me. How was Ashley when she got home?

Disappointed you weren't waiting at the door, but otherwise in good spirits.

I guess I'll have to make it up to her.

She woke up happy this morning. Does that mean Walter will be getting a second date?

She always wakes up happy on her day off.

Day off?

You know what that means?

No, what?

Dog park!

A bunch of strange dogs running around off leash. What could go wrong?

CHAPTER TWENTY-SEVEN

Dog park. A wave of apprehension crashes over me like a bucket of cold water. A trip to the dog park sounds about as appealing as getting sprayed by a skunk. Just when I thought things couldn't get any worse. It's bad enough I have to walk around naked in front of everyone, I don't need a bunch of strange noses up my butt. They're probably all regulars there. I'll stick out like a vegetarian at a barbecue.

Hey Rufus, you've been to the dog park. What's it like?

It's a good time. You get to run around and play without a tether. You'll sniff a lot of new butts and get to know everybody. He looks at me with a dopey expression, like that's a good thing.

I think I'll pass.

Rufus tilts his head. *What?*

Getting a nose full of ass isn't the way I would choose to spend my time.

You might make some new friends.

If that's how the friend thing works, I don't need any new friends.

We're interrupted by Ashley with a couple of leashes in her hand. "Come on you two, we're going to the park."

I rack my brain, trying to think of a way out of this fiasco.

"This is your first time, Stella. You'll have a lot of fun."

Fun? I'd rather kiss a cactus.

Rufus gets up in my grille as Ashley attaches my restraint. *You better start acting like a real dog.*

I couldn't tell if it was a threat or just some practical advice.

When we hit the sidewalk, instinct takes over and I sniff everything in sight.

How am I doing, Rufus?

Bet... bet... ter.

As we head toward the corner, I pull up alongside him. *You okay?*

I don't have to wait for an answer. I see it in his eyes and smell it. He reeks of the same smell I detected earlier. My instincts tell me he's in trouble. *Rufus?*

Instead of answering, his eyes roll back, and he trembles like he's lost control of his muscles. His feet drag and he stumbles.

Talk to me, Rufus. What's going on?

When he doesn't reply, I bark to get Ashley's attention. She pulls on our leashes and Rufus falls to the ground. This gets her attention, and she turns around.

"Rufus!"

She's on her knees, and I give her some room. His eyes stare at some unknown object in the distance as he continues to tremble.

Ashley comforts him with her magic fingers. "It's okay, boy, just relax and breathe."

It's not okay, and I think we both know it.

"Don't worry. You can rest here as long as you need. We're in no hurry." She continues to comfort him. "Please be okay," she whispers near his ear.

We need to do something, but I don't know what. I get the feeling Ashley doesn't either.

I hear the building's front door close and watch Tyler walk down the stairs. Maybe he can help. I bark, but he can't hear me over the traffic. Ashley sets our leashes on the ground as she tends to Rufus. This is my chance to do something.

I run as fast as I can toward Tyler, who is walking in the opposite direction. I'm wheezing like a chain smoker, and my heart is about to burst through my chest onto the sidewalk. He can't see me, so I attempt to bark, but in my present condition, all that comes out is a grunt.

If I stop now, I might lose him, but it's the only way to get my bark back. It's a gamble, but one I have to take. I put on the brakes and take a few seconds to catch my breath. He's getting away. I take a deep breath and throw everything I have into it. The sound that emerges from my mouth surprises me. Three quick barks echo off the buildings like shotgun blasts.

Tyler stops and turns around. "Stella?" He walks toward me.

It worked.

"What are you doing out here alone?"

I give him the sad eyes and a few pathetic whines.

"Where's Ashley?"

Why do people always ask questions when they know we can't answer? I turn, take a few steps, and bark. Tyler frowns as he looks down the block.

"Is that her at the corner? Is she in trouble?"

More questions I can't answer. *Follow me. Hurry!* I run toward Ash and Rufus. Tyler follows.

When we reach them, Ashley is frantic. She tries to comfort Rufus, who is still lying on the ground.

"Did he get hit by a car?" Tyler scans the area. "Was it a hit and run?"

"Tyler. Thank God you're here. I need to get him to the vet hospital."

"What happened?"

Ashley stands. "I think he's having a seizure."

Tyler drapes his arm around her shoulder. She cries, and he comforts her.

"Stella flagged me down at the end of the block. How can I help?"

"I need to get Rufus into my car so I can take him to the animal hospital. They have an urgent care facility."

What? No dog park. I lean in close to Rufus's ear. *Thanks, buddy. I owe you one.*

"I'll get Rufus and follow you to your car."

After Tyler sets Rufus down in the back seat, I climb in and sit next to him.

"I'd go with you," Tyler says, "but I have an appointment."

"That's okay. You've been a big help. I'm sure someone from the hospital can get him inside when we get there."

She gives Tyler a quick hug, and we tear out of the parking lot. Rufus is lying still across the back seat, his eyes open and staring.

Hey, Rufus. You still with us? We're taking you to the hospital to get you checked out. Whatever this is, they'll fix you right up. I'm not so sure that's how it will go, but I know enough to keep my opinions to myself. He needs encouragement right now.

Ash parks near the emergency entrance. "Stella, stay with Rufus while I get help."

A big dude in hospital scrubs carries Rufus inside. I follow Ashley into the exam room.

Rufus lies on a metal table in the middle of the small room. Ashley stops in front of two chairs on this side of the table. The doctor stands on the other side with his hands on Rufus. Ashley describes what happened on the sidewalk.

She's about to burst into tears.

I've never felt so helpless. *What's happening? I can't see anything.* I let out a quick bark.

She picks me up and deposits me in an empty chair. It's better, but Mitch's six-foot frame would be helpful right now.

"From what you described, it sounds like Rufus had a seizure," the doctor says. "He appears to be resting comfortably now."

Ashley is wringing her hands. "What could have caused the seizure?"

"He's getting old, so it could be any number of things."

"Like what?"

"Has he had any chocolate or caffeine?"

"Not that I'm aware of."

What kind of question is that? He's a dog. Wait. He might have had a cup of espresso and a chocolate croissant for breakfast.

"Any poisons around the house he may have gotten into?"

"No. Nothing."

The doctor hesitates. "Let me run some tests and see if we can get some answers."

He doesn't know what's wrong. That can't be good. *Come on, Rufus. You gotta pull through. Do it for Ashley.*

I'm overwhelmed by the moment. *Okay, you big doofus, do it for me, too.*

Chapter Twenty-Eight

After the doctor tells Ashley the tests will take at least an hour, we leave the hospital for a more comfortable place to wait. The coffee shop at the end of the block appears to be where we're headed. Inside, the rich aroma of freshly ground beans hangs heavy in the air and mingles with the warm, inviting fragrance of baked goods. With each step, memories of my former life evoke a sense of longing for the simple pleasures I once took for granted. It seems like a lifetime ago.

I overheard the doctor ask if Rufus had ingested any caffeine, so I know I won't be enjoying any of Mitch's favorite hot beverages. Hmm... perhaps a donut and a cup of decaf? I won't get my hopes up.

A puzzling scent rides along on the coffee laden air. It's familiar, but somehow out of place. Jim? Jim-in-the-box, homeless-shelter Jim? I scan the tables as Ashley leads me up to the counter.

"What can I get for you?"

That's Jim's voice. He works here?

I can't see anything from the floor. I get excited and hop around, throwing in a couple of barks for good measure.

"Stella! Behave."

I continue my tantrum, hoping she'll pick me up so I can get a better look.

"She's a feisty one, isn't she?"

"I'm sorry."

"That's okay." He leans over the counter for a look.

"She's not usually like this."

He doesn't look like Jim. Another sniff verifies my earlier assumption. I try to picture this guy with long hair and a shaggy beard.

"I used to have one just like her."

Wait. What?

Ash picks me up and rests me on her hip like a toddler, and I find myself face to face with my old pal Jim.

I like the new look. I give him a quick bark. You know, to say hello.

Jim studies me.

"I'll have a caramel latte and..." She bends to survey the tempting array of baked goods through the glass.

I'll take one of each.

She straightens up. "Just the latte. Thank you."

What?!

Jim's been staring at me the entire time. He turns to Ashley. "Sure. Coming right up."

I watch him as he steps away to fix her drink. Memories of my time with him flood back. I'm not sure whether he doesn't recognize me or he's still mad that I betrayed him. Either way, I stand by my decision.

Jim sets the latte on the counter. "This is going to sound crazy, but I think that used to be my dog."

It's not something a dog owner hears every day. Ash glances at me, a worried look in her eyes like he might snatch me from her arms and run out the back door. She turns her body to put a little more distance between me and the counter.

Jim smiles. "I know, it sounds like a bad pickup line, but I had a pug named Stella."

He's telling the truth. Hey, Jim. It's me, Stella. I'm that dog.
"Seriously?"

"It's the truth. I had to give her up a few months ago because..." He hesitates. "Well, let's just say I was going through a rough patch, and she deserved better."

"I've only had her for a month."

"The timeline fits."

Ash turns to me. "Well, Stella, do you recognize..."

"Jim," he offers.

I give him another quick bark, and everyone laughs.

"I'm Ashley. It's nice to meet you, Jim. How much do I owe you?"

"Oh, no. Stella's money is no good in here."

"Really?" She pauses. "Is that just today or is it good for…"

Jim chuckles. "Let's not get carried away."

Everyone laughs again.

I turn around as we walk toward the door. Jim says something to a girl behind the counter, then removes his apron.

Ashley pulls out a chair under the awning out front and sets me down. I can tell she's distracted. She nearly spills her coffee before sitting at the table next to me. "What just happened?"

Small world, huh? I hung around with Jim for a while before you and I hooked up. You're not jealous, are you?

"It was a legitimate adoption. You're my dog now."

Roger that. I'm not going anywhere. Till death do us part and all that.

She takes a sip from her cup as she stares at the traffic.

I notice Jim in the window. He smiles and waves when he sees me.

Jim's a decent guy. He wouldn't start any trouble, would he? It worries me that I don't know much about him. I paraphrase one of Bogey's lines from the movie *Casablanca. Of all the coffee joints in all the towns in all the world, we walk into his.*

Yikes! He's headed this way. I bark to snap Ashley out of her trance.

She sets her cup down, stands, and slings her purse over her shoulder. I can smell her fear.

Jim holds up his hands as he approaches. "Please. Wait. I come in peace."

Ashley hesitates. She glances at me, then back at Jim.

"I'm not here to cause any trouble. I just want to talk."

"Okay." Ashley's muscles relax and she sits. Her purse remains on her shoulder, presumably to make a quick getaway if one is required.

"I never thought I'd see Stella again." Jim cautiously reaches his hand out toward me. "May I pet her?"

"I guess that would be okay."

Jim strokes my head and scratches behind my ears, and I melt into the chair. Turning to Ashley, he says, "She likes when you scratch there."

"I can see that."

Jim stops scratching and straightens in his seat. "I feel like I should tell you a little about our history."

What's the matter? You can't scratch and talk at the same time?

"I don't know much about her life before the adoption."

He leans in, forearms on the table, and lowers his voice. "When I first met Stella, I was living in a box under the railroad bridge near Ferry Lane."

Ashley's face registers a mix of shock and disbelief. "You're kidding."

"I believe she came into my life for a reason." He sits back in his seat. "I saved her from a pack of wild dogs that were just about to eat her alive. And in return, she saved me from myself."

You didn't see it that way at first. I'm glad you've come around. So, I guess we're cool.

"I don't understand," Ashley says.

"Believe it or not, I used to work on Wall Street. I fell on some hard times and lost everything, including my home. You can't imagine how scary that was, but I tried to make the best of it. I was embarrassed and too proud to ask for help." He pauses. "Somehow, this little dog understood that and showed me the way back to civilization."

"How did she do that?"

"She called the cops."

"Stella?"

"Led them right to my door. They put us in a homeless shelter."

Wasn't that better than a box?

"At first, I was angry. We'd been together for a while and had become best friends. But her betrayal soured our relationship for me. She stayed at the shelter for a while, under the radar, but I turned my back on her."

Ashley nodded. "My friend at the adoption agency said Stella spent some time in a shelter."

"I watched as the other residents welcomed her and quickly befriended her. I became jealous, and it made me realize that

I'd been wrong. Stella had done me a big favor. I cleaned up my act, and with the help of a social worker, here I am."

"How did Stella end up at the adoption agency?"

"They had rules about pets at the shelter, but the director looked the other way when she saw how much her being there was good for the residents. That is, until some jerk who'd been kicked out for stealing blew her in."

Yeah. Larry. He was a troublemaker.

"What did you mean when you said she was good for the residents?"

"I've come to realize Stella is special."

I am?

"She sat in on our sessions with the social worker," he continues. "Some of those guys were in rough shape, but everyone said they felt more at ease when Stella was around. She was our emotional support. I know it sounds crazy. She's just a dog, but..."

Just a dog?

"It's not crazy. I've felt it, too."

You have?

Jim stands. "Well, I'd better get back. I can't afford to lose this job."

"It was nice meeting you, Jim... and thank you for sharing."

He disappears inside.

Ash turns to me. "You've been holding out on me, Stella." She looks at her phone. "We need to get back to the hospital."

Chapter Twenty-Nine

The waiting room at the hospital is full when we return, but the nurse takes us right in and deposits us in an empty exam room. I'm not sure if that's a good sign or a bad one. I think they do that to give the impression things are moving along smoothly, when all they're doing is making you wait in a different room. Fortunately, I have a poor sense of time. I park myself on the floor next to Ashley's chair and stare at the door. The sound of other dogs whining and barking outside is unsettling. None of them are happy to be here. I don't hear Rufus.

Ashley stands and paces. "I'm worried."

I'm sure he's all right. She can't understand me, so I must be trying to convince myself.

Just before she wears a hole in the floor, the door opens and a tech brings Rufus in. He's walking under his own power and doesn't look any worse for the wear. She hands his leash to Ashley. "The doctor will be with you in a minute."

"Thank you." Ashley kneels and throws a big hug around Rufus as the tech leaves the room. "I'm so glad to see you. I hope everything is okay."

I walk to a spot where he can see me over Ash's shoulder. *IS everything okay?*

I don't know. They put me in a big machine, then stuck a needle in my butt.

Did the doc say anything?

He talked with the one who brought me in here. They said something about a tumor. I don't know what that means.

Yikes! I do, but I don't want to be the one to break the bad news. *We'll have to wait and see what the doc says.*

A few minutes later, the doctor enters the room. Poor Rufus takes a step backward, like he expects another needle jab.

Ashley stands. "How is he, doctor?"

"Please sit. I'm afraid I have some bad news." He pauses as Ash takes a seat. "After a blood test ruled out infection and liver disease, I ordered a cat scan."

A cat scan? Rufus is a dog.

"The scan revealed a large mass on his brain."

"A tumor?" Ashley struggles to compose herself.

There's that word again.

It's not a good word, Rufus. I figure he'd want me to be straight with him. *It means you're sick.*

"He has cancer?"

"Yes. It's called a canine glioma."

"Is there anything we can do?"

"Because of the location and the dog's age, I would recommend against surgery or other heroic measures. The best thing we can do for Rufus is to keep him comfortable. I gave him a steroid shot to help with the swelling and reduce the pressure, and I'll prescribe some anti-seizure and pain meds."

"Is he in pain?"

"He doesn't appear to be, but his condition could deteriorate rapidly."

"How long does he have?"

"Hard to say for sure, perhaps a month, maybe two, depending on how aggressive the tumor is."

"Oh, no." She hugs Rufus. "Poor Rufus."

I envy all the lovin' Rufus is getting, until I remember why.

Rufus turns his head to look at me. *What's going on?*

I'm gonna be straight with you. You're sick, and you've only got a couple of months to live.

Oh. Is that why she's sad?

Yeah. We all are.

You're sad?

Sure. You're a big pain in my ass, but we're family.

Gee, thanks.

The doctor sends us home with some medications and literature on what to expect over the next few months. Ashley loads us into the back seat and sobs as she stares through the windshield.

I put my front paws on the console and stick my head between the bucket seats. *Ash? Are you okay?* It's a stupid question, and for once I'm glad she can't understand me.

She reaches over and strokes the top of my head. "What are we going to do without Rufus?"

I don't have an answer. If she'd asked me a couple of weeks ago, I'd have had plenty to say. But, at the moment, my disdain for the big doofus seems petty and insignificant.

Ashley wipes a tear from her cheek and takes a deep breath. "The doctor said to keep him comfortable, but to act as normal as possible. We don't want Rufus to know there's a problem."

I'm afraid that ship has sailed. I kinda told him. In my defense, dogs can sense these kinds of things, anyway.

"We were on our way to the dog park this morning, so that's where we're going to go."

I feign excitement. *Hey, Rufus. We're going to the park. That sounds like fun.*

I try to think positively. *Yeah, let's go have some fun.*

Something happens the moment we walk through the gate into the park. My inner dog takes over, or maybe I just don't want to spoil Rufus's time here by being a Debbie Downer. The air is alive with the barks, yips, and playful growls of dogs of all shapes and sizes having the time of their lives.

My tail twitches with anticipation as I take in the vibrant scents that ride on the warm air. The earthy aroma of freshly cut grass mingles with the tantalizing scent of treats and the distinct musk of wet fur. Wait. Wet fur?

Ashley finds an empty bench and releases my tether. I run two circuits around the bench while she unhooks Rufus. The endorphin release feels good. *Come on, Rufus. Let's go check this out.*

I'm right behind you.

I feel the joy of a child running through the grass. What's happening to me? My paws kick up sprays of fresh-cut grass as my stubby legs churn, but I'm no match for Rufus, who passes me easily on our race to nowhere. Whoever said "it's a dog's life" probably wasn't a dog.

I see a squirrel out of the corner of my eye and slam on the brakes. I tumble head over feet a couple of times before I come to a stop. Rufus looks back. *What's the matter, first day with your new legs?*

I ignore his snarky comment. *Squirrel!* Instinct takes over, and before I have time to think, I'm chasing it. I forget about Rufus. The only thing on my mind is catching that squirrel. Don't ask me why. I'll never catch him, but that doesn't stop me.

He darts up a tree and taunts me from one of the lower branches. I want to bark, but I don't give him the satisfaction. That, and I don't want to draw attention to my public humiliation. I linger for a moment until I remember Rufus. *Yikes!* I need to get back.

I find him chatting it up with a group of dogs in the shade of a willow tree. I hesitate and turn around to look for Ashley. She's still seated on her bench. Cautiously, I approach the group.

Who's your friend? one of them asks.

That's Stella. She's okay.

I nod. *Hey, everybody.*

This is Bailey, Jack, and Maggie.

I'm surrounded by inquiring noses intent on sniffing my backside. I turn away. They follow. I turn again and find myself face to face, or more precisely, face to butt, with a beagle. I think it's Jack. At this point, I'm holding my breath.

What's wrong with her? Maggie asks.

She's just shy. First time here.

I can't hold it any longer and breathe in. *Whoa!* Instead of a nose full of ass, I get an information dump. It's like I just Googled Jack the beagle. After that, we all take turns getting to know each other in the usual manner.

Rufus speaks. *Now that everybody knows everybody, lets decide on a game to play.*

Everyone agrees except me. *Rufus, I think we better get back.*

What's your hurry? Maggie asks.

Rufus needs to take it easy.

Why? Is something wrong?

No. I'm fine. Stella is just overreacting.

Okay, guys, we need a moment. I glare at Rufus. *Sidebar?*

I nudge him a few steps away from the group. *We need to get back to Ashley. Now.*

Don't get your tail in a knot.

I'm worried if you overdo it out here, your head will explode.

The doctor said to act as normal as possible.

THAT he understood. *Look, if we don't head back right now, I'll tell your friends what's going on.*

Rufus hangs his head in defeat.

I turn to the group. *Sorry, guys, but we need to get back.*

Yeah, we'll get together again soon.

We leave the three staring at us while we head back to the bench.

"There you are," Ashley says. "I was just about to go look for you."

I told Rufus he needs to take it easy.

Look, Nurse Stella, I can take care of myself.

Ashley wags a finger at Rufus. "You need to take it easy, Rufus."

I give Rufus the side-eye. *Told you.*

"Sit over here, and I'll get you a treat."

I'll have one of those, too, please.

CHAPTER THIRTY

R ufus is quiet on the way home. He wants to be mad at me, but I think he knows I'm just trying to help. I have a feeling he's not the only one who will need my help.

I sense a change in the atmosphere when we return home. Sadness hangs in the air like a dense fog. Ashley's once vibrant energy seems tempered with sadness, and Rufus appears more subdued. I don't see how any of us can go on like this for the time Rufus has left. We need a distraction.

As if on cue, the doorbell rings. Ashley's confused expression makes me wonder who it could be in the middle of the afternoon. I run to the door. It's Tyler. I can smell him.

Ashley opens the door. "Tyler."

"I hope you don't mind my stopping by. I'm on my way to work and wanted to check in on Rufus."

"That's sweet." Her shoulders slump and she sighs. "I wish I could say he's fine, but..."

Tyler reaches for her but pulls back.

Don't be shy. She needs a hug right now. I move in closer.

"Hi, Stella." He turns his attention back to Ashley. "What's the matter with Rufus?"

"I don't want to burden you."

That's not true. Well, maybe the burden part, but she needs to talk to someone.

"No burden. I have a few minutes. Can I come in?" He hesitates. "I mean, if it's not too much trouble."

"No trouble at all. It will give me a chance to thank you again for your help this morning."

Once inside, she stands with her back to the closed door, like she doesn't want him to leave. It's subtle, but dogs are highly sensitive to chemical changes associated with different emotions. They are also adept at reading body language. Mitch would have loved to possess that superpower.

He nods. "Just being a good neighbor."

She studies him for a moment without a response.

He continues. "I'm sure you would have done the same for me."

"I guess you're right."

"So, what's going on with Rufus?"

She motions to the couch, and they sit. I curl up next to her feet so she feels my comforting touch. Rufus shuffles over.

"They ran a bunch of tests and found a brain tumor."

"Oh, no." He reaches out to Rufus and scratches behind his ears. "Poor boy." He turns to Ashley. "I'm sorry. That must be a devastating blow."

She nods, her eyes glistening with unshed tears.

"You need a distraction. How about if I cook you a nice dinner?"

"That's very thoughtful, but—"

"Before you say no, I should tell you I'm the head chef at a little bistro downtown. I know my way around a kitchen."

Say yes. Say yes. You know you want to.

Ashley glances at Rufus and me.

Tyler nods his head in our direction. "The dogs are invited, too."

"Then how can I say no?"

"You can't. Tomorrow night? Dinner is at six-thirty, but you're welcome to come earlier for a cocktail, if you like."

Is this a date? Are you seeing this, Rufus?

A silence descends as Ash nervously twirls a lock of her hair.

I sense a strong chemistry between the two. It's lousy timing with the whole Rufus thing, but it might be just what she needs. Her pheromone readings are off the chart. I have to admit, I'm not averse to something developing here.

Tyler breaks the trance. "I need to get going. Don't want to be late for work."

He stands, and Ashley follows suit.

"Thank you again for your help this morning... and for the dinner invitation."

Yeah. What she said.

"My pleasure." He pets Rufus and me. "Bye guys. See you tomorrow."

Ashley ushers Tyler out and stares at the closed door.

So, THAT just happened.

She turns around and the spark of a smile flashes across her lips. Some of the fog in the room clears. "Who wants a treat?"

A treat? For no reason? Perhaps this dark cloud has a silver lining.

Later that night, with Rufus snoring in his bed and Ashley sobbing in hers, I feel the need to do something. I could make some noise and Ashley might bring me into her bed, but—I can't believe I'm saying this—it isn't always about me.

I leave my bed and stand next to Rufus. *Hey, Rufus. Wake up.*

This better be important.

It is. Ashley is sad, and I think you can help.

Okay. What should I do?

Act sad so she can comfort you. I think it will help her more than it helps you.

Rufus climbs into Ashley's bed and whimpers.

"Oh, Rufus." The tears flow faster. "Come here, my good boy."

She pulls him close, sobbing and stroking his fur. He looks down at me with a contented smile. I'd give him a thumbs-up if I had one.

I return to my bed, feeling like a third wheel, but I know they need each other now. I realize being part of a family means helping the other members, even if it requires some sacrifice.

The light of day brings a sudden change in Ashley's emotional state. Perhaps she's focusing on tonight's dinner with Tyler, or maybe the thought of losing Rufus is so painful she chooses to ignore it. Either way, she smiles and hands out treats like she owns stock in the company.

I benefit from her generosity, even as she focuses her full attention on Rufus. We're all in this together, for better or for worse.

Ashley leaves me in charge while she's at work. The day, which is uneventful, drags on in anticipation of a five-star meal at Tyler's place tonight. Rufus had picked up on Ashley's good mood before she left, and it stayed with him the rest of the day.

Ash returns home to find both of us waiting by the door.

Can we go now? I'm getting hungry.

What she said, Rufus barks.

"Aww. You couldn't wait for me to get home."

Okay. Let's go with that.

"Give me a minute to get changed and we'll go for a walk."

I don't want to waste any time, but a walk will free up more room for food. We wait at her bedroom door, leashes hanging from our mouths.

"Wow. Someone's in a hurry to go out."

I pause at Tyler's door and sniff. It's too early to determine what's on tonight's menu, but I can tell something good is happening inside.

The fresh air increases my appetite. Rufus and I dispense with the usual deliberation over the appropriate dumping ground. We take care of business quickly, and let Ashley know of our desire to make a hasty retreat to our building.

Tantalizing aromas greet us in the hall upon our return. Ashley knocks on Tyler's door as we mill around at her feet, ready to charge inside and locate the source. I haven't seen Rufus this excited since he broke the vase and blamed it on me. In the end, restraint wins out for fear of being sent home before the main course.

After what seems like hours waiting for Tyler and Ash to finish their cocktails and small talk, the feeding frenzy begins. The food is so good, I almost miss the smiles and googly eyes going on at the adults' table. It's nice to see Ashley enjoying herself after a couple of difficult days.

I have an idea. Let's all move in together and let Tyler do the cooking. No offense, Ash.

CHAPTER THIRTY-ONE

The next morning, I don't feel so good. I may have eaten too much last night, which would make today's malaise worth it. However, it seems like there's more to it than that. I'm too weak to get out of bed. Ashley stops by on her way to work with a measure of concern and gives me some lovin'.

Rufus shuffles in after she leaves. *What's the matter?*

I feel like crap.

Join the club.

That's not a club I care to join, but it raises the possibility I may already have become a member. I quickly dismiss the thought. *Go away. I just want to sleep for a while.*

Rufus hangs his head and shuffles back into the living room.

I feel somewhat better when I awake again and try to step lively as I make my way into the kitchen to have a late breakfast. I don't want to be one of those dogs who sleeps all the time, like the one in the other room.

If I'd slept through breakfast when I first got here, I would have found an empty bowl when I awoke. But Rufus no longer seems interested in such harassment. It's sad to think he needs a death sentence to bring him around. I guess when you know you're about to die, you take stock of your life—think about the what-ifs and the regrets and try to be better. Perhaps Rufus is one of the lucky ones. Not everyone gets that chance. Mitch didn't.

A week goes by and my energy level hasn't improved. I'm worried I may have caught something from Rufus. Perhaps he gave me a tumor. *Yikes!* I can't die. What will Ashley do? It isn't lost on me that my first thought is not about me, but about Ashley.

I'm turning into one of those annoying, clingy dogs that can't stay away from their master. I follow Ash around like a lovesick puppy and struggle to make it through the eight hours she's at work. When she finally comes home, I whine until she picks me up. Very unbecoming, but I can't help it. My emotions, which I'm just growing into, are all messed up. If there's an upside, it's that Ashley needs comfort and security as much as I do. She's sadder over this Rufus thing than she's letting on.

During the day, I follow Rufus around and sleep next to him. The smell of death is getting stronger. I'm still getting used to the idea that I can smell death on someone, like a ghoul just waiting around to steal the body when they die. It's disturbing, to say the least.

I don't think he has much time. He will never admit it, but he needs someone. I can be that someone when Ash isn't around.

Another week passes before I'm back to something that resembles my old self. Whatever challenged my emotional stability seems to have passed. I'm still sad about Rufus's condition, which seems to be getting worse, and want to do everything I can to make his remaining time as comfortable as possible. But the whining and obsessive neediness have diminished to a tolerable level.

Emotions are something new that I need to deal with. Westcott men never had time for something as trivial as emotions. It's a sign of weakness. Father taught me that. He said God made women to handle the emotional side of things. Men take care of everything else, and they do it with strength and determination. It made sense at the time.

News flash, Stella. You're a dog now. Dogs don't play by the same rules as humans, especially the male variety. They're like children, hopelessly naïve and willing to love unconditionally. It's been a hard pill to swallow given my upbringing. At the moment, that pill is stuck in my throat.

On Saturday, the three of us head to the park. Ashley unhooks our leashes, and I walk with Rufus rather than run off.

We circle the park, taking in the fresh air and the abundance of sights and smells. He strolls along, obviously enjoying the mundane things many others take for granted.

I like the park, Rufus says.

Me, too. I could come here every day.

You don't have to walk with me if you'd rather go run around. You're young. You need more exercise.

Don't worry about me. I'm fine.

I notice our stroll is attracting more than the usual amount of attention.

Not today, guys. Rufus is tired, so we're taking it easy.

Eventually, they turn their attention to other things, and we stop to rest under a maple tree. After a few moments, I notice Rufus's stare.

What?

You're bleeding.

I look down. *Yikes!*

He moves in for a closer look.

This is all his fault! However, I don't recall ever seeing him bleed. Maybe because he has different plumbing. I thought the tumor he gave me was in my brain, not my hoo-ha.

See what you did.

It wasn't me. He sniffs around a bit. *I think you're in heat.*

It's not that warm out. Besides, dogs don't bleed when they get hot.

Now who's the doofus?

The other dogs are back, and they're not taking no for an answer. They're like sharks with blood in the water. I growl and show my teeth, which doesn't scare anybody. A couple of people notice the disturbance and retrieve their pets.

I turn back to Rufus. *I'm not the doofus. This is serious!*

No, it's not. It's natural. But you should stay away from other dogs for a while.

What do you mean?

Let's just say, male dogs grow horns around a dog in heat.

Is that what's going on here? I pause. *What about you?*

Nah. I'm too old and sick to care. Besides, you're not my type.

So, I don't have a tumor?

Probably not. But you might have puppies.

What?! I glance around to see where Ashley is. I'm having a hard enough time being a dog, I don't think I can be a mom, too.

Rufus reclines in the shade. *Ashley doesn't need any more dogs.*

I'm aware. Whatever you do, don't tell her about this.

I CAN'T tell her. I'm a dog.

Two weeks ago, you would have found a way.

He hangs his head. *Two weeks ago seems like another lifetime.*

More dogs are sniffing around.

Has everyone gone crazy? Come on, Rufus, we need to get out of here.

I clean myself up, which is gross, and we head back to Ashley's bench. I need to find out more information about this heat thing. Unfortunately, dogs can't Google.

CHAPTER THIRTY-TWO

Tyler comes over after dinner, and I meet him at the door with my tail twitching. Ashley's been seeing more of him, and I'm okay with that. In fact, they have my blessing. She needs a man—a good man—and I think she's finally found one.

He normally works nights, and Ashley days, but they see each other regularly on their days off. Tonight is movie night.

Hey, Rufus. Tyler is here.

Hi Tyler, he calls from the kitchen. The tile floor is cool, so he spends a lot of time there.

They take a seat on the couch and turn on the TV. If Ash and I were alone, I might get to watch from her lap. But when company is here, I sit on the floor where dogs belong. I get it. Mitch never let Rufus on the couch for movie night. Three's a crowd.

Imagine my surprise when Tyler scoops me up and deposits me on the couch next to Ashley. He sits on one side, and I'm on the other—like an Ashley sandwich. I snuggle up next to her thigh and watch the opening credits. Her magic fingers gently caress my back.

It's a rom-com, Ashley's favorite. Mitch wasn't a big fan. He preferred action flicks like *Die Hard* or *Mission: Impossible*. But I'm just happy to be here.

I've noticed dogs don't see colors like humans, so the screen is bland and more of a sedative than in the past. Halfway in, I give up and close my heavy eyes. They stay closed until the final credits. The music brings me back. I glance at my two companions to find them both awake. Kudos to Tyler, who made it to the end. He's a better man than Mitch.

After some whispers and giggles, Ash sets me on the floor, and walks Tyler to the door for another round of giggles and close talking. That's cute, but the show's over, literally. Give him a kiss goodnight so we can all go to bed.

Wait. What's happening? Wrong door. The front door is that way.

They disappear into the bedroom.

No one told me it was a sleepover.

"Come on, Stella," Ash calls from inside the room.

Hard pass. I need to draw the line somewhere. *I'll sleep out here.*

She stands in the doorway. "Are you coming?"

I whine and cover my eyes with my front paws.

"Okay. Suit yourself."

The door closes.

My paws are sweating, and I have trouble breathing. *Get a grip, Stella. She's a woman and you're a dog. She's out of your league now. It's never gonna happen.* Another hard pill to swallow.

I wander into the kitchen where Rufus is asleep on the floor. I don't think he knows what's going on anymore, if he ever did. I'm a little envious. Given the present situation, things would be easier if I were a little more like Rufus. But there's something I need to know before he checks out.

Rufus, you awake?

I am now.

Was Mitch really that bad?

Pretty much.

Enough to make Ash pick up stakes and move out of town? Who does that?

I think there's more to it.

What do you mean?

Some older guy came around a couple of times, and Ashley got all nervous.

Really? What did he look like?

I don't remember. He had fancy clothes. The last time he turned up, they had a fight.

I'm pacing now. *Is that why she stopped taking my, I mean Mitch's, calls?*

I don't know. He pauses. *Can you stand still? You're making me dizzy.*

Then a few days later, she was gone.

Yeah, it happened pretty fast.

Thanks. You can go back to sleep now.

I guess I'm not over Ashley as much as I thought I was. But Tyler is a good man. I like him, and not just because he can cook. He's exactly what she needs after all those false starts. I need to keep telling myself that.

Rufus snores as I return to the living room.

A man in fancy clothes?

I notice I'm bleeding again and clean myself up, which only adds insult to injury.

After a restless night on the floor, watching Ashley's door and drifting off to sleep from time to time, morning arrives. She emerges dressed for work while Tyler sneaks out the front door. They're not fooling anybody. I close my eyes as she passes me on the way to the kitchen.

Rufus spent the night on the kitchen floor. With one eye open, I watch Ash step over him to get her breakfast. Eventually, he wakes, and she talks to him. She shows him some lovin', which is enough to get a wag or two, but not enough to get him up off the floor.

Our bowls get filled before she walks past me to the door. She must be running late. Her goodbyes echo through the apartment just before the front door closes. She's too distracted to notice what I can sense. Rufus is dying, and I'm afraid I might have to spend the better part of the day alone with his corpse.

As soon as I'm sure she's gone, I shuffle over to Rufus. *I'm going to have some breakfast. Why don't you join me?*

I'm not hungry. His eyes move, but his head never leaves the floor.

Come on, man, you gotta eat.

You eat. I'll watch. I'm just gonna lie here for a while.

Suit yourself. I'm hungry, so I empty my bowl and chase it with some cool water.

Maybe you need some exercise to get the ol' blood flowing.

Maybe I don't.

I hang my head. I know he knows what's happening here.

Please let me die in peace.

You can't die yet.

Why not?

Do you really want THIS to be the last face you see?

You've got a point.

If you insist on dying today, you need to wait until Ashley comes home.

I'll try.

I lie down beside him. *I'll just hang with you here for a while. We can get some exercise later.*

Okay.

Maybe we can go to the park tomorrow. Not something I care to do, given the bullseye on my back. But Rufus needs something to look forward to.

A silence descends on the room. I let it be, not knowing what else to say. Sometimes, just being there with someone is worth a thousand words.

After some time, I feel Rufus shivering. *Are you cold?*
A little.

I glance at the blanket on the couch. *Stay here. I got you covered. And I mean that literally.* Not even a smile from Rufus. *Tough room.*

Upon closer inspection, I find the edge of the blanket just out of reach. Standing on my little hind legs does no good.

My previous attempts to leap onto the couch ended in disaster, but desperate times require desperate measures. I back up, take a deep breath, and get a running start. I hit the front of the couch like Wile E. Coyote running into a rock wall while he chases the roadrunner. It feels like slow motion as I slide back to the floor with the end of the blanket in my teeth. Tiny stars swirl around the edges of my vision as I drag my prize to the kitchen and drape it over Rufus.

Thank you, Rufus whispers. *As much of a tool as Mitch was, everyone has love and compassion inside. Sometimes they need a different perspective to let it shine.*

I assume he's referring to me and appreciate his kind words. He's not such a bad guy, after all. Whatever happened in the past doesn't matter. He may be a big doofus, but he's my big doofus, and I love him.

I lie down beside him to offer additional warmth and the comfort of knowing he's not alone. The afternoon is spent by Rufus's side, drifting in and out of sleep and listening for his heartbeat now and then. Relief washes over me when I hear the front door open.

CHAPTER THIRTY-THREE

"**I**'m home," Ashley calls.

Rufus's heart beats slowly, but it's still beating. I look at him. *You made it!*

We're in here, I shout. I'm sure all she heard was a bark.

"What's going on in there?"

When she sees us on the floor, she drops to her knees beside Rufus. "What? Rufus, are you okay?"

His eyes follow her movements, but he remains on the floor.

Ashley turns to me. "The blanket?"

That was me.

She glances back at the couch. "How did...?"

It wasn't easy. But Rufus needed help.

Tears roll down her cheeks. "We need to get him to the hospital."

After some pleading and prodding, it's clear Rufus won't be going anywhere under his own power.

Ashley grabs her phone from her purse, dials, and waits. "Tyler. I'm glad I caught you. Are you still home?"

She pauses and her shoulders slump. "Oh."

What did he say?

"I found Rufus on the floor when I got home. He can't get up. I need to get him to the hospital."

Another pause. "Thank you, thank you." She ends the call and wipes away her tears.

"You're a good friend, Stella. I'm glad Rufus didn't have to do this alone."

She gently strokes Rufus's head. "It's going to be all right."

He looks up, and his tail moves in a weak wag. We all know it isn't.

"You can rest here. Help is on the way."

Ashley stands. "Come on, Stella. We need to get ready to go. Tyler will be here in ten minutes."

When Tyler arrives, he scoops up Rufus and carries him to his car parked out front. "I'll drive you to the hospital."

On the way, Ashley thanks Tyler between her tears. "What about work? I don't want you to get into any trouble."

"They can manage without me for a few hours."

We stop in front of the emergency entrance. Tyler instructs Ashley to go inside and let them know we're here. She grabs me out of the back seat, and we run inside and flag down a nurse to explain our situation.

The front doors slide open, and Tyler walks in. He looks bigger than I remember, and reminds me of a picture I'd seen of a firefighter rescuing a frightened child from a burning building.

A nurse ushers us into an exam room, where Tyler sets Rufus on the table. She asks a bunch of questions, then tells us the doctor will be in shortly.

Ashley thanks Tyler again and says she'll understand if he needs to get back to work.

"How will you get home?" he replies.

She offers up a blank stare. "Oh, yeah. I'm sorry. I can't think straight."

"I have to move my car. I'll take Stella and we'll wait for you in the waiting room."

Why do I have to go? I look around the room and realize this isn't about me, so I go quietly.

With the car parked in the designated lot, we sit in the waiting room. Tyler makes nervous small talk, but I can't keep my eyes off the exam room door. Eventually, Ashley emerges. She's alone, the tracks of her tears still fresh on her face.

The mood is somber on the ride home. I can't believe Rufus is gone. Tyler walks us to the apartment door, but says he needs to get back to work.

"I can check in on you later, if you like."

"I appreciate everything you've done for us. I'll be okay. Stella is here with me."

Yeah. I got this, Ty.

When he leaves and the door closes, I feel an emptiness like something, or someone, is missing. I sense Ashley feels it, too. Rufus's scent is everywhere and won't be going away for a while. We should probably clean up his toys that are strewn around the apartment, but not tonight.

Ashley sits on the couch with me on her lap like she must have done a hundred times with Rufus. She sobs as she strokes my back and stares at a black TV screen. We don't have a history like she had with Rufus, but sometimes a warm body and a little compassion are enough to keep the heartache at bay. I've discovered dogs are uniquely qualified to provide such comfort.

The morning light finds us snuggled up on the couch. Ashley rises, puts some food out for me and gets dressed. She's not wearing her work clothes, so I assume she's taken the day off. I'm relieved. I was not looking forward to spending the day alone, with no one to talk to or chase me around and break stuff.

After an unusually quick walk—Rufus used to slow us down—we return to find Tyler at our door with coffee and donuts. Ashley thanks him and ushers him inside. Before they sit, Tyler pulls a donut from the bag and places it in my bowl.

Glazed. My favorite. This one's a keeper, Ash.

Her body language suggests she agrees. I don't pay much attention to their conversation until I hear my name.

"Stella did that."

What? What did I do?

"So, you didn't put the blanket over Rufus?"

She shakes her head. "Somehow Stella pulled it off the couch and covered him up before I got home. I found them both on the floor together."

"I'm not surprised. Dogs are often used as emotional support animals. They can sense sickness and emotional distress and become a source of compassion and healing energy."

"I've heard that." She pauses. "I ran into a guy named Jim who works at the coffee shop near the vet hospital. He claims Stella was once his dog. Apparently, they spent some time in a homeless shelter where Stella provided such support for many of the men there."

"Maybe you could put her to work at the hospital."

What? We can go to work together? I gotta tell you, it's no fun here alone all day. I'm in.

"The children there would love her."

Tyler finishes his donut and chases it with the rest of his coffee. "She might require some training, but it doesn't hurt to ask."

"I know they have dogs come in from time to time for the children. I'll ask around."

"I think she'd like that."

"There's also a hospice care center at the hospital. Given the way she was with Rufus at the end, it might also be a good fit."

"Sounds like a plan."

They stand, and it appears our little coffee klatch is over. Ash walks Tyler to the door, and I follow him out into the hall.

She likes you, Ty. Don't be a stranger.

CHAPTER THIRTY-FOUR

I spend the afternoon lounging around the apartment, picturing myself walking the halls of the hospital, wearing scrubs and tripping over my stethoscope. I understand scrubs now come in many colors. My favorite color is blue.

It must have been a dream, because Ash had never mentioned my work attire. I'll probably wear what I always wear, which I'm a little embarrassed to admit is nothing. But scrubs would be a nice touch.

I'm not sure why I'm so excited about having a job. Maybe because Mitch never worked a day in his life so this will be a new experience. It's not like a real job, and I don't expect to get paid. That would be ridiculous, right? But I enjoy helping people— something else Mitch never did—and from what I've heard, that's the extent of the job description.

It's getting late in the day and we're out for a walk so I can make room for dinner. I thought if I had Ashley all to myself, I would feel better, but I miss Rufus. I remember my first week living with them and how badly I wanted him to be gone. All I can say is, be careful what you wish for.

Another sad night in the apartment. Ashley flips through channels for a while after dinner, but nothing seems to interest her. She skips right over *Groundhog Day* with Bill Murray. I, well, Mitch, used to think it was funny how Bill relived the same day over and over in the movie. However, that storyline lost its luster when I started waking up every morning as a dog. Okay, not exactly the same thing. My situation is much worse.

We sit in silence together for a while before I follow her into the bedroom. She lets me sleep in the bed with her. I guess every dark cloud has a silver lining.

In the morning, we take a quick walk, then I slam my breakfast and wait by the door. Here she comes now, all ready for work. I love a chick in uniform.

"Be a good girl, Stella. I'll be home in time for dinner."

Wait. What? I'm going with you, aren't I?

The door closes, and I take it as a big, fat NO. I'm confused. I thought we would ride together. What am I supposed to do now, take the bus? I'll be late. Wait a minute. What exactly are my hours? We're going to have a chat when she gets home tonight.

The apartment feels bigger as I rattle around in it, feeling forgotten and alone. I could break something so she doesn't trust me here by myself. Then she'd have to take me with her.

Either that, or send me back to the adoption agency. Not a gamble I'm willing to take.

When in doubt, take a nap. I know it doesn't rhyme. I'll have to work on it. There's a nice warm spot near the window where the sun shines in for most of the morning. Rufus had seniority, so it was his spot. *Who's the top dog now?* Sleep comes easily and lasts until the sun is overhead and no longer shines through the window.

I wander into the kitchen to see if Ashley left me anything to eat, but all I find are two empty bowls. She often left us treats to get us through the long afternoons. She hasn't picked up Rufus's bowl yet, and I don't know if it's an oversight or it's too soon. I'm okay if she leaves it, as long as she fills them both.

With nothing else to do, I begin my vigil near the front door. I don't know how long I'll have to wait because I'm losing the ability to read a clock. Telling time is now based on auditory events, such as the sound of the mail truck around three o'clock. I haven't heard him yet today.

I'd kept certain human traits while I was younger, such as reading, telling time, and chasing women. But as I've grown, they've given way to more canine instincts. My sense of smell and my hearing are so much better it's ridiculous. I've also noticed I can't pass by a squirrel without giving chase. I'll probably never catch one and don't know what I would do with it if I did.

I can hear her footsteps in the hall—smell her, too. The door opens.

"Hi, Stella. How was your day?"

It still amazes me that people ask dogs questions they can't possibly answer. *Could have been better if I'd started my new job today.* I notice she has something in her arms. Perhaps to make up for leaving me behind this morning. *Is that a present for me? We can talk later.*

She walks right past me and sets it on the coffee table. I follow her and give it a sniff. I hope that's not dinner in there. It's burnt.

"It's Rufus's ashes."

And they're on our coffee table because...?

"Now he can stay with us forever." She turns the box to expose a picture of Rufus stuck to the front.

I think it's a little creepy. *Did anyone check with him before they tossed him in the fire and boxed him up?*

The following day, I'm home alone again, but it's worse than the day before. I glance every now and then at Rufus's photo on the box. He says nothing, just stares. His eyes follow me around the room all day.

I realize too late how nice it was to have him around to talk to, even if he said a lot of dumb things. It makes me wonder if we need another dog, but I quickly dismiss the thought for two reasons. First, it's too soon. And second, it gives me more alone time with Ashley.

Speaking of Ashley, she should be home soon. It's been a while since the mailman was here. With Rufus watching, I take up my position by the door. I stand when I hear her. My tail vibrates like a cell phone. I can't help myself or understand why I act like this. She dissed me the past two days. I should chew her slippers, but instead I'm happy to see her, ready to shower her with affection. It must be a dog thing.

"Hi, Stella." She sets her purse down and drops to one knee. "How would you like to come to work with me tomorrow?"

I thought you'd never ask. No, really. That's what I thought.

Chapter Thirty-Five

Today is a good day. The sun is out, my belly is full, and I'm standing on the back seat with my head out the window on my way to work.

"I told everyone at work you were a good dog and have had prior experience, so don't make me look bad."

I'm not sure that's possible. You looking bad, I mean.

"You'll be meeting with Erin, the pediatric program coordinator. She'll observe you today to see if you're a good fit."

It sounds like a job interview. I thought the position was mine.

"If she likes you, you'll get to meet some of the children."

Children? Dogs LOVE children.

We stop at a light near the park. *Is that a squirrel?* My frantic attempts to climb out the window are unsuccessful. I shake my head to clear it. *Stella! Focus.*

"When we bring animals in, it really raises the children's spirits. Some of them are very sick."

You know I'm not a doctor, right?

Ashley pulls into the parking lot of a large building. "We're here."

Inside, the air is sterile. The odor of disinfectant is tempered by a hint of freshly laundered linens. I'm confused and disoriented by the cacophony of sounds—hurried footsteps, beeping medical equipment, and a dozen different conversations. This is not how I pictured my new work environment. My initial reaction is to tank the interview so we can get the hell out of there.

Perhaps I was a bit hasty about this whole job thing. But I'm committed now. Ashley is my ride, so I follow her down a long hall and onto an elevator. We get off on the second floor. There's a different atmosphere here, and I'm pleasantly surprised if not relieved. The disinfectant scent is softer, and the walls are adorned with colorful pictures that evoke feelings of innocence and hope.

As we walk down another long hall, I see children. Some are in rooms and others in the hall. Two young ones in the hall squeal with delight when they see me. This is encouraging, and I give them a playful bark.

"Stella! Shhh."

Really? What was I supposed to do? They started it.

A large woman with silver hair and too much makeup steps out of an office and greets us.

"Hello, Ashley." She pauses and takes a long look at yours truly. "And this must be Stella."

Her voice and her hands are gentle as she picks me up. She has a sweet tooth. I know because her hands smell like chocolate. I lick them and look at her with my big googly eyes, and she can't look away. They're mesmerizing, I know, and I've learned to use them to my advantage.

She sets me down while she speaks with Ashley. They talk about a training program for therapy dogs. *Therapy dog. I like the sound of that.* I can see it engraved on a plaque on my office door.

Apparently, they want to observe me in the field to see if I might qualify for the training. *No problem. I got this.* I sniff around a bit before I sit and watch them trade comments like I'm watching a tennis match. My eyes couldn't be any googlier.

Before she leaves, Ashley stoops and strokes my back. "I need to get to work. You be a good girl for Erin. She's going to show you around and introduce you to some children."

Sure thing, Ash. You're coming back to get me, right?

She leaves, and I'm alone with Chocolate Hands, or CH, as I call her. I sit and wait for her to show me my new office. Eventually, she leads me toward a room where the voices of children spill out into the hall. My tail twitches with excitement.

Inside, a handful of children play, but the mood is not as upbeat as I'd imagined. Some sit quietly at small tables, coloring or working on puzzles. Others read or watch TV.

I sense they are sick, but they seem content, at least for the moment.

They stop what they're doing when I enter and run toward me. Their smiles fill me with delight, and I can barely stand still, but the boss is here, and I don't want to blow it on the first day. They pet and scratch and hug like they've never seen a dog before.

Slow down, kids. There's enough of me to go around.

CH hands me off to a younger woman with long brown hair pulled back into a ponytail. She's dressed in scrubs and smells like coconuts. She smiles and leads me to a spot in the middle of the room, then directs the children to sit in front of me. Everyone obliges except a boy named Josh. He stands with his arms folded across his chest.

The other children think he's a troublemaker. I'm sure there's more to it than that. I sense he's having a difficult time accepting his illness and would rather be anywhere else.

"Dogs are stupid," he says.

Of course, I could be mistaken.

The door opens, and a nurse wheels a little blond-haired girl in and parks her off to the side. She's another one who doesn't look excited to see me.

Nurse Coconut introduces everyone. I have the difficult task of learning seven names, eight if you include the one in the wheelchair, while everyone else only has to remember

Stella. It's my first assignment, and I don't want to screw it up.

"Stella will be here at the hospital for the next couple of weeks to play with you."

The room gets loud again, and Nurse Coconut claps her hands. "Quiet, children. I'm going to let Stella wander around and visit with each of you until lunch. Please be patient. Everyone will get to spend time with her."

The crowd disperses except for a couple of boys who hang around. They pet me and ask stupid questions, like if I can fetch. *Of course I can fetch. All dogs can fetch. It's in our DNA.*

I glance over at the wheelchair. The girl stares at me, her expression unreadable. *Excuse me gents, I need to take care of something. I'll be right back.*

I sit directly in front of her wheelchair. The girl's eyes hold more than a child's share of sadness.

I noticed you staring at me. Is there something you'd like to say?

"No. I didn't even want to come down here."

That's funny. It sounded like you answered my question.

"Why is it funny?"

My heart rate quickens. *Everyone knows people and dogs can't talk to each other.* I pause to catch my breath. *You can understand me?*

She nods.

That's incredible. Have you always been able to—

"You're not even a dog, are you?"

Yikes! Does she know about Mitch, too? *Of course I'm a dog. Why would you say that?*

"You have a curly tail. Like a pig." A flicker of a smile flashes across her lips.

I bark. *There. Pigs can't do that, can they?*

Nurse Coconut calls out. "Stella!"

I glare at the girl. *Are you trying to get me fired?*

She pauses for a moment. "Maybe."

Let's start over. What's your name?

"I know YOUR name." She crosses her arms.

She's getting on my last nerve, but I stop short of telling her what I really think of her. She's probably a good kid in a bad situation. I'm here to help these kids, not judge them.

So why don't you want to be here?

"I've seen dogs before. And all of them are cuter than you."

Okay. That's enough for now. *I need to spend some time over there with the others.* I can't keep myself from taking a parting shot. *Where I'm appreciated.*

I mill around and play with the other children, but I can't help glancing from time to time at the sad little girl sitting alone on the other side of the room.

Just before lunchtime, I wander back over to the wheel-chair. *You're staring again. What is it?*

The nurse who wheeled her into the room is back. "We need to get you something to eat."

"I'm not hungry."

I watch them head for the door.

The girl leans over the side and turns back toward me. "My name is Hannah."

This one is a real project.

CHAPTER THIRTY-SIX

Nurse Coconut says it's time for my break. It must be an OSHA thing. We ride the elevator downstairs and walk outside to a small fenced-in yard with grass and a couple of trees.

There's another dog working here, a terrier, I think. He passed me in the hall earlier, and I thought he was kinda cute. I don't know where that came from or why I said it. I haven't been feeling myself lately. He wore a little jacket that said "Therapy Dog." Ya gotta love a dog in uniform.

A few minutes later, a nurse drops him off in the yard. I remember Rufus had said I was hot and should stay away from other dogs, but it's kind of hard to do here.

As soon as he spots me, he comes sniffing around. *You're new here.*

Maybe I am.

Just wanted to welcome you to the team. My name is Rudy.

Okay, then. I'm Stella.

He's obviously been through the program. Perhaps he could give me a few pointers. But Rudy is rude and gets all up in my personal space. I take a couple of steps backward. Ashley had played hard to get with Mitch, but it just made him try harder. Rudy closes the gap, and I find his alpha behavior oddly attractive. What am I thinking? This is all very confusing. My canine instincts overpower my common sense.

We dance around each other for a while in some kind of mating ritual. It isn't my idea. I'm playing defense, deflecting his advances as best I can, but I don't know how long I can keep him at bay.

Then, I smell it—coconuts. *Saved by the smell!* Nurse Coconut opens the door and calls my name. Break time is over.

See you around, Stella.

I do what any self-respecting female in my position would do. I thrust my chin in the air. *In your dreams.*

I'm counting on it.

She attaches my leash, and we head back upstairs.

Where do I find the HR Department? I want to file a complaint against one of your employees.

When we return to the second-floor activity room, I find a different group of children. They converge on me with similar enthusiasm. Hannah is not among them. I can't stop thinking about her, wondering what brings her to this hospital. Her eyes are almost as big as mine, but they don't shine like other children I've seen. They're guarded.

I move about the room, stopping to spend time with each child, feeling their anxiety lessen with each stroke of my fur. I glance at the door from time to time to see if Hannah might come rolling in. She doesn't. I want to go look for her, but I need to be here for the ones who showed up.

I know I can do good work here. These children need someone who will listen with undivided attention to the things they can't say out loud to anyone else. I can be that someone. Dogs are like antidepressants without the side effects.

One by one, the children head back to their rooms. It must be near quitting time. One boy, I think his name is Ethan, remains. With his bald head and round glasses, he reminds me of a miniature Howie Mandel. He kneels in front of me and sits back on his heels. I rest my chin on his thigh and look up at him while he strokes my back. No words are spoken.

"Thank you, Stella," he says after a long silence. "I hope you come back to see us again."

You can count on it, my friend.

CH enters the room, and Ethan says goodbye.

"It looks like you've made quite an impression on Ethan."

I made a few friends today. I want to ask about Hannah, but she wouldn't understand.

"Tomorrow, we'll visit the hospice care center to see if you can make some friends there."

I know what that word means, and after Rufus, I'm not sure I'm ready for that. *Okay, but when do I get to see the children again?*

She waves her chocolate hand in front of my face, and I want to lick it, but she's too quick. She attaches my leash and leads me downstairs.

I'm back outside in the yard with Rudy.

"You can play out here while Ashley finishes her shift. She'll be along shortly."

Not shortly enough.

I watch her leave, aware Rudy is closing in on my position. I turn to him. *What's your problem?*

He stops abruptly. *Hello to you, too, Stella.*

I'm taken aback for a moment, but I sense his remark is more sarcasm than sincerity.

No problem. I just want to talk, he says after the obligatory sniff.

That's what Mitch would say. I used to be that guy. We never just wanted to talk.

Rufus warned me this heat thing I'm going through is like a dog magnet. Unfortunately, he never said how long it would last. I love working here and don't want to let this Casanova jeopardize my employment. Perhaps I could take my breaks in the break room with the other employees.

Okay, let's talk. You go first.

He doesn't know what to say.

I thought so.

Come on, Stella. I know you're in the mood. I can smell it a mile away.

Must be the heat thing again. Despite my stupid little legs, I decide to run. It doesn't take long for him to catch me. And if you don't mind, I'd rather not talk about it.

"Boys will be boys," they would say when Mitch acted like that. You don't want to know what they said about the girls.

I hear Ashley shout, "Get away from her."

Rudy runs away as she approaches.

"Did he hurt you?"

Just my pride.

"Come on, it's time to go home."

It was time to go home ten minutes ago. Where were you?

CHAPTER THIRTY-SEVEN

The following day, Nurse Coconut takes me up to the fifth floor and past a sign that reads "Hospice Care." I'm pretty sure they're trying me out in various settings to determine the best fit.

I notice a different atmosphere as soon as we walk in. The children I saw yesterday were young and still full of hope, something that is in short supply here. Nevertheless, I have a job to do.

There's no activity room. Everyone pretty much stays in bed. Death is in the air, and I can sense the anxiety that accompanies it. I hope my presence can offer a peaceful distraction, not only to the patients, but to family members as well.

Today, Coconut—we're on a first-name basis now—provides a brightly colored vest for me to wear. The words "Therapy Dog" are missing because I haven't earned them yet. I assume the adults I'll work with today would be more suspicious than the children about unmarked dogs wandering around the halls of the hospital.

I'm anxious—not the best frame of mind for a therapy dog—as she leads me into the first room, which looks more like a hotel suite than a sterile hospital room. I didn't know what to expect, but it wasn't this. The bed, adorned with crisp white linens and plump pillows, is the focal point of the room. Its occupant lies still and serene. Her tired gaze follows me into the room. She smiles, and I take a deep breath. *You got this, Stella.*

The patient is not alone. A thirty-something woman, a granddaughter perhaps, stands by the bed engaged in quiet conversation, her face etched with a mixture of grief and acceptance. Another, much younger visitor—a child of ten or twelve years, with tear-stained cheeks—sits in one of the upholstered chairs.

I wander over to the child and nuzzle her leg. She picks me up and sets me on her lap.

"What's your name?"

"Her name is Stella," Coconut replies.

"That's a pretty name." She looks up at Coconut. "Can she stay for a while?"

"Absolutely. She helps people who are sad feel a little better. Perhaps your grandmother would like to hold her when you're done."

The girl is busy stroking my fur, but her mother nods. I glance at Grandma and notice her stare, her wrinkled face twisted into a smile. Coconut promises to check back later, then leaves the room. I'm alone with this grieving family I just met. Amidst the somber backdrop, there's a palpable undercurrent of warmth and compassion that fills me with a sense of purpose.

Eventually, I end up in bed with Grandma. She has a gentle touch, and whispers to me in a language I don't understand. The scent of death is all around her. I want to tell her everything will be alright. Unless she comes back as a dog, but even that hasn't worked out too badly for me. So, I comfort her with the warmth of my body and the unconditional love dogs naturally exude.

Coconut returns just before I fall asleep with Grandma. I need to find out if sleeping on the job is frowned upon. While this type of work is emotionally draining for most humans, dogs take it in stride. Of course, when I miss the two or three naps I've grown accustomed to every day, something's got to give.

I spend the rest of the morning in another room with another family. Same situation, different people. In patients who are near death, I sense a fear of being judged for their actions. A healthy dose of canine unconditional love lessens their burden.

Break time follows, and I find myself alone in the yard. Rudy never shows, and I wonder if Ashley said something to someone in management.

When my break is over, it's back to the hospice wing for more comforting and perhaps a nap. When we enter the next room, I realize there will be no naps in here. The shock of seeing my, er, Mitch's, mother in a chair near the bed is enough to keep me awake for the rest of the day.

There could only be one person occupying that bed—the father I'd spent years despising, the man I would have been happy to never see again. I freeze, unsure of what to do. I didn't even know he was sick. My mother's sad expression brightens a little as she watches me, and I almost run to her, but memories of that man hold me in place.

I don't know where to go, but I can't stay in this room. At the risk of losing my job, I turn toward the door and pull the leash from Coconut's hand as I scamper out into the hall.

"Stella! Come back here."

She apologizes to my mother before giving chase. I don't lose Coconut, just let her know it's time to move on. There must be more rooms to visit, more sick to attend to.

Apparently, I wasn't clear enough because she gathers my leash and attempts to lead me back inside. I whimper and stand my ground. It becomes a tug-of-war, with neither side willing to concede defeat. Any growl or bark will earn me a pink slip, so I continue to whimper, which attracts attention.

Finally, Coconut concedes and leads me to the next room. At the end of the workday, we stop by CH's office to report.

"How did she do with the hospice patients?"

"I don't know why, but she refused to stay in one of the rooms."

I have my reasons.

"Which room?"

"The patient's name was Mitchell Westcott II." She pauses. "We moved on, and she was fine after that."

I wasn't fine. Seeing him again brought too many bad memories rushing back.

One in particular is unsettling. I'm in Father's study telling him about Ashley's sudden disappearance.

"You've never had a problem attracting women. There will be plenty more, I'm sure."

"Ashley was different."

"Don't be silly. Women are all the same."

I'm no expert, but he's clueless when it comes to women. I don't know how Mother put up with him for so long.

"Good talk."

I've always blamed Ashley for my untimely demise that night, unwilling as I was to shoulder any blame myself, but Father had as much to do with it as anyone.

"Perhaps she's better suited to working with children," CH says.

Roger that.

CHAPTER THIRTY-EIGHT

After a restless night, I push aside the memories of Father so I can be there for the children. I admire their enthusiasm, even as they face a variety of difficult health issues. They lift my spirits as much as I seem to lift theirs, and I look forward to our time together.

Apparently, my meltdown the day before in the hospice wing has caused management to rethink my usefulness in that venue. I spend the next few days on the children's floor with no mention of the word *hospice* by anyone. This, of course, is fine with me.

Other than the aforementioned blemish on my record, I feel positive about my first week on the job and the prospect of training to become a therapy dog.

Ashley is off for a couple of days, and I enjoy our time together around the apartment, but the communication gap is frustrating. Even though Rufus wasn't the sharpest knife in the drawer, when he was here, I could engage in a little two-way communication. The silver lining, if there is one, is that Ash will sometimes tell me things she ordinarily wouldn't say out loud to anyone.

I'm curious how she feels about her past relationship with Mitch. She doesn't talk about him, and I'm in no position to ask questions. Previous conversations I've overheard seem to indicate it's not all bad. Imagine if she were to discover the truth about her little doggie.

Tyler stops over to pick up Ash for a trip to the market. He'll cook dinner here tonight, after which I assume there will be a quid pro quo sleepover. I've gotten used to the idea. I have little energy today, so I plan to nap while they're out.

I awaken upon their return to see Ashley in the kitchen, staring at my food dish.

"Stella. You haven't eaten. Are you feeling okay?"

I wander into the kitchen and whine. The smell of the steaks Tyler is putting in the fridge doesn't even excite me. This, of course, is cause for concern.

"She'll come around when she smells dinner," Tyler says.

Ashley stares at me with nervous eyes, and I know she's remembering Rufus.

I wander back into the living room, lie down, and tell myself it's not a tumor.

***

I return to work after the break, anxious to see Hannah again, but she's a no-show. I'm worried about her and desperate for some information. Taking advantage of a distraction in the room, I slip out into the hall.

I walk like I own the place, hoping anyone I run into assumes I know what I am doing. The first room I check is empty, probably belonging to one of the children I left behind in the activity room. I move on to the next and the next and the next.

I notice an empty wheelchair in the fifth room and peek inside. A woman smiles at me from a bedside chair.

Hannah sits up in her bed, eyes wide. "Stella!"

My search is over. I hear Nurse Coconut in the hall as I stroll inside. I scamper under the bed, look up at the woman with my big, sad, please-don't-tell-them-I'm-here eyes, and step backward into the darkness to wait.

"Mama, shhh," Hannah says.

A few minutes later, I hear the door close and watch the woman return to her seat.

"The coast is clear," Hannah says.

When I step out from under the bed, her mama picks me up and deposits me into Hannah's open arms.

With my tail wagging to beat the band, I lick her face until she giggles. *I missed you, Hannah Banana. Are you okay?* I stop for a moment, then lick her again.

Her smile turns to a frown. "Not really."

What's the matter?

"I get tired easy and can't always catch my breath. That's why I haven't been able to go to the activity room."

Mama watches us with a curious expression.

You should go. I hear they have a dog down there who looks like a pig.

Hannah giggles. "Yeah, she's not very cute, is she?"

The girl has a sense of humor. *I... I thought you didn't like me.*

"I was just having a bad day."

Her mama is on the edge of her chair. "Hannah? What are you doing?"

"Talking to Stella."

Mama smiles. "You have a vivid imagination."

"It's not my imagination. She can talk."

"I don't hear her."

"Dogs don't talk out loud. I can hear them in my head. Like I have headphones on."

"Are you saying all dogs talk?"

"I don't know, but all the ones I've met do."

Tell her I'd like to thank her for not ratting me out to the nurse. Maybe I can shake her hand.

"She says thanks for not telling the nurse she's here."

Don't forget the shake.

"Oh, yeah. She wants to shake your hand."

Mama stares through squinted eyes. "Stella said that?"

I hold out my paw and she blinks back her surprise.

She takes my extended paw and gives it a little shake. "She does seem rather intelligent."

Lady, you have no idea.

The door opens and Coconut walks in.

"There you are."

Hannah pulls me close and squeezes me. "Please don't take her yet."

Coconut hesitates, then glances at Mama.

"You should have seen her face light up when Stella walked in," Mama says. "Perhaps you could let her stay for a little while."

"I guess that'll be okay. I'll be back in a half hour."

"Thank you," Hannah says. "I'll take real good care of her."

Likewise, I'm sure.

Funny thing. After Coconut leaves, Mama speaks to me like I'm just another one of Hannah's little friends. I learn Hannah has been sick for most of her life with a bad heart. I don't understand the medical jargon, just that she is waiting for a heart transplant.

When Coconut returns, she promises to bring me around again for a visit if Hannah isn't feeling up to a trip to the activity room. With that assurance, I agree to go peacefully.

I'm mobbed when we return to the activity room. Apparently, Josh had started a rumor that I'd escaped, run into the road, and was hit by a car. My resurrection proves to be the highlight of their day. When the hoopla dies down, I notice several of the children park themselves in one corner and pay homage to a blue dog on television. *A blue dog? What are they teaching kids nowadays?* I tell myself he's only a cartoon, but I don't like the competition. The other children get a little extra lovin' just in case.

The afternoon flies by, and I can't believe it's quitting time when Coconut shows up. She leads me downstairs to the yard where Ashley will pick me up. I talk most of the way, but she ignores me. In her defense, she doesn't speak my language.

I want to tell Ashley all about my day on the ride home, but once again, I'd be wasting my breath. It's times like these I miss Rufus. Perhaps getting another dog isn't such a bad idea.

With all the excitement of the afternoon, I don't realize how tired I am, and fall asleep as soon as we get home. I sleep through dinner, which elicits concern from Ashley. When I fail to finish my food, she launches a barrage of questions I can't answer. She's not the only one with questions as the tumor talk resumes in my mind.

I feel somewhat better in the morning and make a valiant attempt at breakfast in an effort to alleviate her concerns. But after a long day at the hospital, I repeat last night's performance, and Ash is talking about a trip to see the vet. It's enough to make me return to the kitchen and choke down the rest of my food.

The remainder of the work week is more of the same, and I look forward to a couple of days off. I'll miss the children, but I need the extra nap time. Instead of a trip to the yard at the end of the last day, Coconut leads me down the long hall to drop me off in CH's office. I sit quietly in the corner and wait for whatever is about to happen.

Ashley arrives and we get started. Apparently, it's time for my performance review. I get mostly good grades, and they both seem pleased. I will be assigned to the children's floor after I complete my training. My excitement is tempered by the fact that entry into the program requires a physical exam and all the requisite shots.

After leaving CH's office, I'm tired and have trouble keeping up with Ash. I've felt a bit off for almost a week, and I now fear it may have something to do with my last encounter with Rudy rather than a tumor.

We make it to the elevator as the doors open. A familiar voice calls out from inside.

"Ashley?"

We are both speechless for a moment.

"Mrs. Westcott. What a surprise."

"Please. Call me Meredith." She pauses. "Are you going up?"

"No. We're on our way down to the garage. I'll get the next one."

The doors begin to close, but my mother stops them and steps off the elevator. "Then I guess we'll have to catch up here."

CHAPTER THIRTY-NINE

Yikes! We should have taken the stairs.

"I'd heard you moved, but I didn't know where," Meredith says.

Nobody did.

"Yes, I'm in Fairfield now."

"I always liked you. I thought you and Mitch made a delightful couple."

I thought the same thing.

Meredith frowns. "We missed you at the funeral."

Ashley shifts her weight to her other foot. "What are you doing in the hospital? Are you okay?"

"I'm fine. It's Mitchell. He's in hospice."

"That must be difficult for you."

These two had always gotten along, but I sense tension on Ashley's part.

Meredith looks down at me. "And who is this?"

"Oh. This is Stella," Ashley says. "She works here with the children."

"We've met."

"You have?"

"Unfortunately, we were never properly introduced before she ran out of the room."

"She ran?"

"Took one look at Mitchell and headed for the door."

"I don't understand."

"Mitchell has often had that effect on people," Meredith says with a wry smile. "And apparently now it extends to dogs, as well."

Roger that.

The doors open and she steps aside to let a young man pass. "Ride up to the fifth floor with me. If you have time, that is. I'm sure Mitchell would love to see you again."

That's a terrible idea. Unfortunately, I'm on the wrong end of the leash.

"I really don't think he wants to see me."

Meredith's expression falls. "Nonsense. Why would you think that?"

"I didn't know him that well, and he didn't get along with Mitch."

That's an understatement.

"The apple doesn't fall far from the tree. They didn't get along because they were so much alike."

I beg your pardon. That is SO not true.

The doors open, and Meredith steps inside. She turns. "Please? He doesn't have long to live."

Ashley hesitates before we follow her.

Hopefully, he'll be dead by the time we get there.

"He was different after Mitch died," Meredith says when we're alone. "It really affected him."

It sure did. He got to keep my trust fund.

"It affected all of us."

Aww.

"Mitchell has a lot of regrets that I'm afraid he'll take to his grave."

Regrets? He wouldn't know a regret if it crawled up his pant leg and bit him on the pecker. If I were taller, I'd be stabbing the button for the parking garage. We get off at the fifth floor, and I lag behind.

Ashley tugs on my leash. "Come on, Stella."

I'm back in his room, and the smell of death is stronger than the last time. My canine instincts take control, and I feel a wave of sympathy for the man. A kinder, gentler memory surfaces.

I'm back in his study, but this time I'm seven years old. "Hey, Pop, it's time for dinner."

"Come over here," he says. "Dinner can wait."

I oblige, and he sets me on his knee. His desk is the size of a small island, his study the command center of his sizable empire.

"Someday, kiddo, this will all be yours."

"Wow!"

"You need to study hard and listen to everything I say."

"Sure, Pop. I want to be rich like you."

I shake my head to clear it. Those days are long gone. I stopped calling him Pop a few years later. I wasn't his kiddo anymore once I started to think for myself and derail his plans.

He was a force to be reckoned with back then. I barely recognize him now. He's lost half his body weight, and his skin is loose and gray. The eyes that once burned hotter than a wildfire, smolder in their sockets.

"Mitchell, look who's here."

He stares at Ashley for a moment. His eyes widen, and I can't tell if it's recognition or terror.

"It's Mitch's girlfriend, Ashley."

She says it like they're still a thing and Mitch is outside parking the car. Meredith misses his reaction. He knows who she is. Meanwhile, Ash is squirming in her compression socks and cross trainers, which confirms my suspicion he'd somehow meddled in my affairs.

"Mitch? Is Mitch here?"

Nice try, old man. He's deflecting.

Ashley's back stiffens. "No, sir, it's Ashley. The one you paid off to break up with Mitch."

What?!

Meredith gasps and covers her mouth with her hand.

Ashley turns to her. "I didn't take his money." She places her hands on the end of the bed and glares at him with accusing eyes. "So he ran me out of town."

Okay. Let's all just take a breath. I certainly need one.

Meredith stands. "Mitchell?"

Tears roll down his hollow cheeks.

"I'm sorry," Ash says to Meredith. "But you're the one who made me come up here." She's crying now. "I had a feeling something like this would happen if I ever saw him again."

I nuzzle her leg. *I'm so sorry, Ash. I didn't know.*

"We all know Mitch had flaws." She turns to Meredith. "Like you said, the apple doesn't fall far from the tree. But Mitch didn't deserve this." She walks to the side of the bed and looks down at the dying man. "I shouldn't have let you bully me, but Mitch's death is on you."

Yikes! My heart is breaking for both of them. More for Ash, but I sense that feeling responsible for his son's death is one of Father's biggest regrets. My inner Mitch wants to tell him to stick his regrets up, well, you know where. But I can't bring myself to do that anymore. Being a dog has taught me a great deal about love and relationships. These were lessons Mitch was unable to learn on his own.

Meredith approaches Ashley, and they embrace. "I'm sorry. I had no idea."

"I didn't want to leave, but he threatened my career."

"If I had known what he was doing, I would have—"

"It's not your fault."

After a tearful few moments, they disengage. "Come on, Stella. We need to go."

"Ashley, dear, will I see you again?"

She hesitates. "I don't know."

"We both loved Mitch. Perhaps we can help each other."

We leave the room without further comment.

I watch Ashley's shoulders heave during the long elevator ride to the parking garage. If I had a voice, I'd tell her Mitch never stopped loving her. He understands she did what she had to do. Now, she's stood up for herself and confronted her demon, and the truth has set her free. Mitch would be proud.

I feel a sense of relief knowing the truth. In a way, it has set me free, as well. I've made my peace with the man. Dogs don't judge, and they don't stay angry. Inner Mitch, on the other hand, has a little more work to do.

CHAPTER FORTY

I stay close to Ash for the rest of the day and into the night for emotional support. She needs a shoulder to cry on, but for some people, a faithful dog with a warm body and a sympathetic ear can work just as well. We spend the night together in the big bed.

Ashley takes the following day off from work. She appears to be feeling better, and we go for a ride in her car. She never mentions the word *vet*, but I'm pretty sure that's where we're headed. I assume it's for the pre-employment physical CH had mentioned.

The doc is a nervous little man with bushy eyebrows and coffee breath. I'm nervous myself, but being able to continue my work with the children will make all the poking, prodding, and needle pricks worthwhile. When he's done, I'm the one who needs a shoulder to cry on. He promises to send the results to CH in a couple of days.

On the way home, we stop at the dog park. I notice I have a little more energy, but I stay close to Ash to offer moral support, and because I still appear to have a target on my back.

Tyler is waiting for us when we return and offers to take us to lunch. We dine outdoors, and Tyler feeds me scraps under the table. I like Tyler despite the increased frequency of his sleepovers. It's obvious Ash likes him, too, so I'm happy for her.

We're back to work the following day. Ashley presses the elevator button, and I pray Meredith isn't on the other side when the doors open. I suggest we take the stairs, but Ash ignores me. The elevator is empty, and we proceed to the second floor. I look forward to the distraction the children provide. I wish Ash could stay and play with us. She could use a distraction as well.

I'm mobbed when I enter the activity room. Even Josh joins in, but I don't see my girl, Hannah. I spend the first hour making sure everyone gets a sufficient dose of Stella. When I make the rounds again, I notice I'm alone with the children, so I slip out the side door. My vest allows me to wander the halls until I find Hannah's room.

Her door is open, but her eyes are closed. I hesitate before entering. Her eyes open as I approach.

Hi, Hannah. Did I wake you?

"No. I was just resting."

Are you alone?

My mom is outside talking to my daddy on the phone.

Did they find you a heart?

"Not yet. It has to match."

I'm sure they're having trouble finding one big enough.

She shrugs.

Are you okay? You seem a little sad.

My daddy was supposed to visit today, but he can't come.

I'm sorry. I lower my head. *My father is sick. He's going to die.*

"Are you sad?"

Honestly, I don't know how to feel.

"I love my daddy. I would be sad if he died."

Our relationship was complicated. I guess he brings the Mitch out in me.

"What?"

Long story.

"I don't know what that means, but you're a dog. Dogs love everybody."

I look up at her, head tilted. *You're right. I've just recently discovered that.*

"People should be more like dogs."

Out of the mouths of babes, right?

"I wish I was a dog."

I love this kid. *Go ahead and ask me again if I'm sad.*

"Are you sad?"

Yes. I'm sad I might never get a chance to tell my father I forgive him.

"What did he do?"

I think about it for a moment. *He wasn't a good father.* After another moment, I add, *But I guess he did the best he could.*

"Then you don't need to forgive him."

What just happened here? *You're pretty smart for only five years old.*

"Five and a half."

Excuse me. Five and a half.

Her mother returns, and Hannah asks her to put me on the bed.

"Maybe you should rest, dear."

"Stella can rest with me."

Sounds like a plan.

We spend the next hour napping, all warm and cozy in her hospital bed.

"I thought I might find you here," Coconut says.

Busted. I'm not ready to go, but duty calls.

"Can I see Stella tomorrow?" Hannah asks.

Coconut smiles. "Sure, honey. I can bring her tomorrow around the same time."

After my required break alone in the yard—I haven't seen Rudy since that first day—I resume my work with the children. It doesn't feel like work when you're having this much fun.

At the end of the day, Coconut leads me down the hall to CH's office, where Ashley is waiting. Coconut closes the door and takes a seat. This looks serious.

CH shuffles some papers on her desk. "I received the results of Stella's exam, and we have a little problem."

Ashley leans in. "Oh, no. Is Stella sick?"

I'm sure she's still sensitive after Rufus's passing.

"Fortunately, no. She's rather healthy... and pregnant."

Honestly, I'm a bit relieved it's not a tumor. On the other hand, yikes!

"What? How did that happen?"

"You're a nurse, Ashley. You know how something like that happens."

"Yes, of course, but I... I had no idea."

"Well, it's true, and I'm afraid we'll need to wait until this clears up before she can enter the program."

Clears up? She makes it sound like I have acne.

"My recommendation for the program will have to wait until she is ready to return to work."

Why can't I work while I'm pregnant? Isn't that discrimination?

"The children will be disappointed," Coconut says. "Can't she stay on for a couple more weeks? I'll monitor her health."

"She's already been through the standard two-week assessment period."

"What's wrong with giving her two more? We'll get an even better assessment. After that, she can have the necessary family leave, then start the training when she returns."

CH thinks about it, then turns to Ashley. "Any objections?"

"None here."

I'm still trying to wrap my head around the pregnancy thing.

CHAPTER FORTY-ONE

"Oh, Stella," Ashley says after we finish dinner. "What are we going to do with you?"

I hope it's a rhetorical question. First, because I have no idea. And second, because I can't speak.

"You know we can't keep a bunch of puppies, right?"

I'm aware. It's not like I planned this. Can we keep one of them? We could use another dog around here. Wait. How do we decide which one?

"I don't know anything about taking care of a pregnant dog, let alone newborn puppies. Tomorrow, I'm going to buy a book."

Good idea. I want to read it after you. Wait. That won't work. Maybe you can read it to me.

"Maybe Tyler will take one."

Let's not count our chickens, er, puppies, before they hatch.

The following day, Coconut brings me to Hannah's room, as promised.

Hey, Hannah Banana. Feeling better today?

"A little."

I have some news. I'm going to have puppies. The idea has been growing on me, or, you might say, in me.

Her face brightens. "Wow! Can I have one?"

Of course.

"Mommy, Stella is going to have puppies."

"Really? She told you that?"

Hannah nods. "She said I could have one."

"Oh, honey, I don't know."

"Pleeeeeeze?"

"We don't have to decide right now, do we?"

Hannah checks with me, then shakes her head.

"Okay, then. I'll have to discuss it with your father."

You think he'll say yes?

She whispers in my ear. "I'm pretty sure I can talk him into anything right now."

My tail flaps like a broken shutter in a hurricane.

With that settled, we move on to the petting and scratching part of the program. Hannah is still waiting for a heart. I want so badly to help her, but what can a dog possibly do? The only thing I can think of is to be there for her while she waits. So, that's what I plan to do, at least as much as my situation will allow.

Being a dog has its benefits, but it has some serious drawbacks, as well. I'd like to be able to come and go as I please. I used to hop in my car and go wherever I wanted, whenever I wanted. Now, I need to rely on someone else to take me outside to poop.

What will Hannah do when I'm out on maternity leave? Wow, that's not something I ever thought I'd say. I blame Rudy for that.

I have two weeks left, so I'm going to make the best of it. The first week flies by. As if Coconut can read my mind, she brings me to see Hannah every day. I spend the rest of my time in the activity room.

Hannah is full of questions about the puppies. When are they coming? How many will there be? What will their names be? And a dozen more I can't answer. She's way more excited than I am. My emotional state is more of an uncomfortable mix of excitement, ignorance, and terror.

Her mother watches with amusement. I can't get a good read on how much of this talking dog concept she believes. I may have to come up with a backup plan to make sure Hannah actually gets one of the pups.

At home, Ashley is reading the book she bought, but as yet has shared very little, which makes me nervous. She treats me differently—feeding me new food, taking me on shorter walks, and spending more cuddling time on the couch. That's all good, especially the last one. She also mentioned a whelping box, which I hope refers to where I will have my pups, and not the sounds I'll make as they arrive.

On our day off, we visit the vet, Coffee Breath gives me a thorough exam, and I mean thorough, and reports to Ashley that I am doing well. We anticipate the blessed event will take place in about three weeks. This is getting real.

I begin my final work week with less energy than the week before. Some would say I'm beginning to show. I say I'm getting fat, and the extra weight is taking a toll. In the activity room, I find a comfy spot and let the children take turns coming to me rather than the other way around. Coconut still brings me to Hannah's room every day.

Tomorrow is my last day, and I don't have a backup plan in place for Hannah's pup. Presently, we only have the word of a five-year-old girl who says a dog promised her one of its pups. I'm afraid that's not enough.

Ashley picks me up from the activity room now instead of the yard. Coffee Breath says I should stay away from other dogs, and we don't want to take a chance horn-dog Rudy might make an appearance.

When we get to the elevator, I keep walking.

Ashley tugs on the leash. "Stella. Where are you going?"

I've got one more thing to take care of before we go home.

She gives the leash another tug, but I won't take no for an answer. I muster whatever strength I have left and take off running. The leash slips from her hand, and she gives chase. I beat her to Hannah's room and duck inside.

Hannah sits up in bed. "Stella! What are you doing here?"

Ashley catches up. She apologizes to Hannah's mom, then looks at Hannah. "You must be Hannah. I understand Stella's been spending a lot of time here."

"Did she tell you that?" asks Hannah.

After a bit of hesitation, Ash smiles. "No, the nurse who brings her down here told me."

This is Ashley.

"You're Ashley?"

Hannah's mom smiles like she recognizes the name.

"Yes, I am. How did you know?"

"Stella talks about you all the time. She really likes you."

An awkward silence hangs in the air.

Tell her how I said you can have a puppy.

"She said I can have one of her puppies."

Ashley frowns and sits on the edge of the bed. "How did you know she was going to have puppies?"

"She told me that, too."

Ashley looks to Hannah's mom for help, but only gets a shrug.

With my head in her hands and her curious eyes gazing into mine, Ashley speaks. "You talked to Hannah? How is that even possible?"

I'm not sure, but it might have something to do with the fact that I was Mitch in a past life.

Ashley stares, unaware of the bomb I just dropped. *Oh, well.*

Hannah, on the other hand... "Who is Mitch?"

Ashley turns and stares at Hannah for a moment before glancing at her mom.

Mom shrugs. "You wouldn't believe the conversations they have."

"I used to date someone named Mitch. How would she know that?"

"Stella mentioned him a few minutes ago," Hannah says matter-of-factly.

"That's impossible." Ashley's face twists into a puzzled expression. "That was before I got Stella. She wouldn't know him."

This is getting weird. I'd better keep my mouth shut.

Another awkward silence.

"Never mind." Ashley smiles and takes Hannah's hand in hers. "If Stella says you can have a puppy, then I'll make sure you get one. That is, if it's okay with your mom."

"Thank you. Then I can have my very own little Stella who can stay with me forever."

Who wouldn't want that? Right?

Chapter Forty-Two

After dinner, we're on the couch watching *Modern Family*. That Cam is a hoot, isn't he? Suddenly, Ashley mutes the television.

Hey!

She turns to me. "What's with you talking to Hannah? Why don't you talk to me?"

I do. All the time. People aren't supposed to hear me. I guess she's special. Oops! That didn't come out right. You're special, too, Ash. SO special.

"Did you just say something? Because I didn't hear it."

I bark.

"Oh, forget it."

The next day is a half day because I have a vet appointment in the afternoon. I arrive at work in the morning with mixed feelings. It's my last day for a while, and I'll miss the children, especially Hannah, but I look forward to the break. I'm tired and feel as big as a whale.

One thing I'm not tired of, is feeling the love from the children. Today it's unmistakable, however there's an undercurrent of sadness running just below the surface. I imagine they will miss me almost as much as I'll miss them.

I park myself in the middle of the room like a beached whale. One by one, they check in with well wishes and some affectionate scratches and petting. More than a few tears are shed, including a couple from Josh, who once told everyone in the room that dogs are stupid. *How do you like me now, Josh?*

Each day at eleven, Coconut brings me to Hannah's room for our daily visit. It's eleven fifteen, and that hasn't happened yet. I'm worried I might not get to say goodbye to my best friend. I'm about to make a fuss when the door opens and Hannah rolls in, holding a bunch of balloons. Coconut enters from the other door with treats for everyone.

It's a party, and this dog is the guest of honor. Everyone gets a big cookie. Mine is a special doggy cookie, and it's delish.

Aww. You shouldn't have. But I'm glad they did. It's nice to feel you make a difference in someone's life, especially a child's. This job is the best thing that has ever happened to me, and I can't wait to start my official training when I get back.

My favorite part of this affair comes after all the treats have been consumed. Coconut lines us up for a photograph. With

Hannah's chair in the middle, and me in her lap, Coconut snaps the photo I will cherish.

After everyone disperses, I look up at Hannah. *I hope you're not here when I get back.* That doesn't sound right.

What I mean is, I hope you get your new heart before then, so you'll be able to run and play outside with other healthy children your age. No more hospitals.

"That will be nice, but I'll miss you."

I'll miss you, too. Maybe I can come visit.

While the children are at lunch, I spend some alone time in the yard. But it's not the children I'm thinking about. Inner Mitch is lobbying to go see his father one more time. I tell him it's not a good idea, but he won't take no for an answer. He says he has one more thing to say. I get it, but the man won't be able to understand him, so why bother? Mitch doesn't care. He has to say it anyway.

I check the door for signs of Ashley. She's coming to pick me up, but I don't know when. Against my better judgment, and because I'll never hear the end of it if I don't, I sneak out of the yard and follow someone into the building. Since I can't reach the elevator buttons, I'll need to climb four flights of stairs—no easy task with the extra weight and these midget legs.

An idea hatches, and I head for the elevator. I follow the next person onto the elevator and ride with him up to the third floor, eliminating half my climb.

I locate the stairs and begin my climb. By the time I reach the fifth floor, I'm wheezing like a rusty harmonica. I stop at the landing for a moment and wonder how I would have climbed the additional two flights. Still wearing my vest, I venture into the hall and walk with purpose so anyone who sees me will assume I'm on official business.

When I step into Father's room, my heart races, and I'm wheezing again. The room is empty, and the bed is made up with fresh linens. I see nothing to indicate he was ever there. I wonder if I have the right room. Inner Mitch is devastated. Whatever he'd planned to say will have to wait... forever, or perhaps for another lifetime.

Nothing to see here. Let's go, I say to Mitch.

Wait.

No. Ashley will be looking for us, I mean ME. Good grief, now I'm talking to myself.

A nurse stands in the doorway. "What are you doing here?"

I panic until she bends down and scratches behind my ears. *That feels good, but I need to know where the man who was in here has gone.*

"I've heard about you. You're Stella. I thought you worked on the second floor."

I'm lost?

"Did you know Mr. Westcott?" She pauses. "I'm sorry to have to tell you, but he passed away yesterday."

This is the right room. *Sorry, Mitch.*

The nurse moves on, and I follow a woman to the elevator and slip in behind her. She gets off at the first floor, and I scurry off toward the yard.

Ashley meets me at the door with a curious look. "There you are."

I'm ready. Let's go.

I spend the next week napping a lot and feeling like I'm coming down with something. What I'm coming down with is motherhood, and it's freaking me out. Ashley introduces me to the whelping box, which is just a big cardboard box with some soft bedding in the bottom. She says I need to get used to it, so I'm spending a lot of time there. I can think of worse places to be.

Ashley has a couple days off, then takes a couple more just before the pups are ready to hatch. I haven't gotten all the lingo down yet, but you know what I mean. She refers to her book often, and sometimes reads aloud to me.

Yikes!

When the blessed event is upon us, I'm panting and wheezing like a broken kazoo. I'll spare you the gory details. Suffice it to say, watching four little creatures squeeze out of me was a sobering experience. They can't open their eyes, and they look more like rodents than puppies.

The four blind mice, as I call them, stumble around in the dark for a couple of weeks. They spend all their time eating, sleeping, and snuggling for warmth. I've never been a mother before, but I'm happy to give them whatever they need.

As I watch them jockey for position at feeding time, I remember when that was me. Being a dog changes a person. That's not a sentence you hear every day. I realize how crazy it sounds, but people and dogs are wired differently. What dogs lack in brain power, they make up for in emotional intelligence. Humans can learn a lot from dogs. I know I have.

Soon, they look like pups, each developing their own personalities. Luckily, three of them resemble their father more than me. The fourth, well, he has my condolences. I notice he keeps to himself more than the others and acts like the odd man out.

I approach as he sits by himself in the corner. *What's the matter, kiddo?*

The pup's head snaps around, and he looks at me with shock and surprise. *Mitch?*

My legs weaken, and I have to shore myself up to keep from falling.

His googly eyes get googlier. *That was you at the hospital? Pop?*

* * *

A Note from the Author

Thank you for investing your valuable time in reading my novel. I hope you enjoyed the story. Please take a moment to visit **www.davidhomick.com** for more information about me and my books and to sign up for my mailing list using the button at the top of the page. You can write to me through the site if you're so inclined. I'd love to hear from you.

Word of mouth is the most powerful promotion any book can receive. If you enjoyed this book, please tell your friends. A shout-out on your favorite social media sites would be cool, too.

I want you, the reader, to know that your review is very important to me and to others that may be considering buying this book. Please consider leaving an honest review on Amazon. It doesn't have to be long, just a sentence or two. Your comments are greatly appreciated.

Thank you, and I wish you all the best.

BOOKS BY DAVID HOMICK

Karma Dog: Unleashing Redemption

Changing the Station: How One Stray Dog Found Its
Purpose

Don't Curse the Rain (Rain Mystery Trilogy Book 1)

Rain Dance (Rain Mystery Trilogy Book 2)

Fire and Rain (Rain Mystery Trilogy Book 3)

From Time to Time

Broken Angels

Reason to Live

www.ingramcontent.com/pod-product-compliance
Lightning Source LLC
Chambersburg PA
CBHW022122310726
48972CB00007B/2160